Gifts of the Heart

Eddie Jane Gavin Pelkey

Eddie Jane 1999

PUBLISHED BY WINSTON-DEREK PUBLISHERS, INC.
Nashville, Tennessee 37205

Library of Congress Catalog Card No: 91-68090
ISBN: 1-55523-503-4

Printed in the United States of America

To my dearest mother,
Edna Helene Gavin, who taught me to love books,
and my dear father,
Caloway Burr Gavin I, my mentor.

Fall cleaning was underway. James had cleaned the basement and the garage. If it were ever possible for these two places to be spotless, this was one of the times. Spring was the other.

My own chores were done, too. This year I had hired a cleaning service to help with the first and second floors of our big old farmhouse, saving the attic for myself. I always enjoy cleaning the attic. Some folks think that I am a little weird because of this preference, but as for me, I like to poke around in the nooks and crannies at the top of the house.

Actually, I never felt I had done justice to this area. That's really why I hired the cleaning service to do the rest of the house. Once and for all, I wanted to be able to spend the time to go through all the trunks, and closets, and old chests of drawers, in the entire third floor. It was my dream come true. In the twenty years that James and I lived in this house, the attic was the last stronghold of our parents' possessions.

My mother died five years ago. His parents were still alive, and up until six months ago lived with us, in this very house. A lot of people couldn't understand how we could get along so well, but then James' parents are different sort of folks. Anyway, enough of that kind of talk, because this story isn't about our family life, it's about me getting to know myself a lot better.

It was while I was cleaning that I found the old boxes. Actually, I knew they were up there somewhere, but I had lost track of them. And besides, I always thought of somebody else's old boxes as being full of treasures, never gave thought to my own as being valuable.

I recognized them immediately. One of them contained my wedding dress. I didn't need to open it to remember the creamy color of the off-white satin. I could envision the cloud of veil drifting around my face on that long-ago day. It had been windy but mild. A warm and gentle sun filtered through the half-grown leaves, dappling the soft grass. The wedding pictures were taken on that very lawn in front of this house.

The other box was tied with string. My fingers trembled as I picked open the knots. Inside, wrapped in layers of tissue, were the treasures of my childhood. I had forgotten how lovely some of these objects were. Often I have heard the phrase "beauty is in the eye of the beholder." I know it's true. I'm sure anyone else looking at these same pieces of memory would wonder what the fuss was about.

On the top were a few toys, relics of my babyhood, and a set of child's silverware. My baptismal clothing and a few baby clothes were the next layer. Beneath these, wrapped in a heavier layer of tissue, was a green-and-red plaid dress with velvet trim and handmade lace. Nestled within the folds of the dress, was a packet of faded letters and a Lapis Lazuli necklace.

My heart jumped. A vision of myself, so real I could almost touch it, clouded my sight. I sat down next to the box and opened the letters. They were in chronological order, starting with the first one. I read.

6 January, 1959

Dear Mother,

Well, I'm here! I still don't know why I had to come to live with your brothers, but I did get here safely. Yes, I slept all right on the train, but *no,* I wasn't comfortable. This town is also really bad. I thought you told me your brothers owned a big store here. This town isn't big enough to have a big store. It's nothing like Chicago. I don't think I'm going to like it here at all, but then, I don't suppose you and Dad care. I hope you have a good time in Europe while Dad studies old tombs.

Uncle George Lee seems okay, but your other brother, Jimmy Burr, seems real odd. He's always muttering to himself. You didn't tell me Talbotsville was named after your family, either. The Talbots of Talbotsville sound pretty gruesome to me. How come, you never brought me down here before this? I didn't even know these two uncles existed.

The other thing, I saw some of the kids at the drugstore. We had to stop and pick up my allergy medicine there. Boy, these kids are nothing like the kids at home. They look like something straight out of *Huck Finn,* and did I get some funny looks. So I said to one of them, "Take a picture; it'll last longer!" Uncle Jimmy Burr got real angry at me, but Uncle George Lee said, "Don't be hard on the child. It's not so easy on her, either." He does seem kind of nice.

Well, I'm tired tonight, but I promised I'd write. So I did. Write to me, too.

Love and Kisses,
Amber Lee

25 January, 1959

Dear Mother,

Uncle George Lee says to say "Hello!" so I am. Really, I don't know why he can't write. He says Jerusalem must be nice this time of year. Lots of sun and warm breezes, and how are the fig trees?

I told him if he has anything else to say, he needs to write himself, I'm not his news agency. He's laughing at me. I don't think it's one bit funny. Well, we have snow. It snowed the day after I got here and it hasn't stopped since. I've never seen so much snow, as a matter of fact. It's so high that we were housebound for several days. I didn't get to start school until the 12th of January.

School is something all right. Mother, you should have told me what this was going to be like. I can't go to a one-room school. I can't concentrate on anything. You always hear what the other grades are doing. There's no privacy to think. You know how I like to think. Well, I can't here! This is a terrible place. I feel like I'm in Purgatory. (In case you didn't know it, that's a new word I learned here. One of my classmates is a Catholic!) When she talks about Purgatory, it sounds just like this school! Mother, couldn't you send me some other place to live? My friend Judith, in Evanston, said I could live with her. You always liked her. What would be wrong with living there while you're gone to the Middle East?

Another thing. Kids here come to school without any socks on under their shoes. No one seems to think anything about it. Golly, people don't even dress right here, Mom. Can't I go back home to live? I could even stay with our housekeeper. Can't you think about it anyway?

I met all the kids in my school. It's easy, we're all in one room, but there are thirty-two of us. One of the grades only has two kids in it. It's real strange. There is one good thing. We're having a spelling bee. You know I'm good at that, so I'm planning on winning it. My only competition is one girl. Her name is India Ingrid. She also told me her mother was your best friend when you were growing up. Is that true?

I met our next-door neighbor, too. Old Mrs. Ruffles. Oh boy! She's really different. She makes good cookies, but she calls them fairy slippers. She says she got the recipe from the Queen of the Fairies. It's strange talking to her. She talks about the birds and animals in the woods like they're real people. She says her pattern for queen's lace trim was a gift from the wood spiders. Weird, Mom. Real weird!

Well, I'm gonna go now. I have a lot of homework to do and I've got to practice my spelling. Uncle Jimmy Burr said he will help. He's kinda strange, too. He gets mad at me real easy, but Uncle George Lee stands up for my sake.

Love and Kisses,
Amber Lee

27 January, 1959

Dear Mother,

Usually I don't write this often 'cause it's a lot of work, but my new friend India Ingrid showed me a picture of you and her mom. It was taken at the school picnic for sixth grade. You looked just like me! Wow! How come I never saw this picture before?

It seems to me that you should have told me about this place. I asked Uncle George Lee about it. (He seems to be friendlier than Uncle Jimmy Burr. Does Jimmy Burr hate me, or what?) Anyway, Uncle George Lee just said there was a little disagreement in the family and you left home. If you ask me (and you're clearly not), I don't blame you one bit for leaving this one-horse town. Mom, it's not even on the map of Illinois. Where is this place? I feel like I'm in Siberia! Well, I have to close now. I just thought I'd tell you the picture was neat. India Ingrid said we could get another copy.

I'm studying hard for the spelling bee.

Love and Kisses,
Amber Lee

1 February, 1959

Dear Mother and Father,

How are you both? Actually I am quite fine. I figured I'd better write and tell you that I really am all right. I know Uncle Jimmy Burr is sending you a special delivery letter 'cause I'm on Penicillin. I know he's going to tell you how bad I am and that I'm an ingrate and all that kind of stuff. I'm really not, but I guess I really, truly was bad and didn't do what I said I would do. What I didn't do, of course, was come right home from school. We stopped over by Miller's Pond and ice-skated. It was just going to be for a little while, but then we forgot the time, and then I fell through the ice. I guess that's why Uncle Jimmy Burr thinks I'm an ingrate (not bothering to think how they would worry about me, I guess). Anyway I'm in bed with a fever and pneumonia. I had to ask the doctor to spell that so I could write to you and tell you what was the matter with me.

All the kids think it's pretty serious, India Ingrid and her brother Jimmy came by to see me. Her mom sent cookies, but Uncle Jimmy Burr said I couldn't have any, 'cause I had been bad and disobedient. What a bother! Uncle Jimmy Burr made Mrs. Ruffles come over and rub my chest with mustard plaster. Oh boy! This is really old fashioned. Even the doctor says so. And, do I ever wish I hadn't gone skating. I'll never do this again!

I have been keeping up with my schoolwork. Mrs. Ruffles snuck me some of her Fairy Slipper Cookies in, when she came to rub my chest. Thank goodness not everyone is crabby like you know who.

I'll write again next week. Can't you come get me? I hate it here.

Your Loving Daughter,
Amber Lee Johnston

Well, I'm in trouble again. This time, surprisingly, it's with Uncle George Lee. They took me down to the store. All I said was, "So this is a General Store. I thought everyone said it was a big store. Why, this is the size of a cracker box. It's nothing like Marshall Fields in Chicago."

Uncle George Lee actually asked me if my mother had forgotten to teach me manners when we were living in the *big city!* Really, Mother, it is a small store. I don't understand what the big fuss is all about. It does have a back room with tools and plumbing supplies, and there is a balcony section where the ladies' department is, but it's still a small store. Haven't they ever been to the *city?*

I don't have any friends here, either. India Ingrid is all right, but she's not like Judith. Boy, I got a letter from her yesterday. They went to Field Museum in Chicago on a field trip. I'll bet down here these teachers don't know what a field trip is. I know it sounds like I'm complaining a lot, but this place is a hick town compared to Evanston. When are you coming home? I can't believe Dad's got to stay there for over a year. I could live there with you. Anything would be better than this burg!

I still plan to win the spelling bee. Our teacher told us there is a wonderful prize. So I'm getting ready. I work on it every night. Uncle Jimmy Burr hasn't stumped me yet. He tried with *picturesque.*

I told him, it's not the long words that are hard. It's the little ones like the word *merely.* Remember that time I just couldn't remember how to spell it and lost the spelling contest? Oh well, write to me. And thanks for the pretty necklace of Lapis Lazuli. It's really very pretty.

8

I really love you very much.

Your Loving Daughter,
Amber Lee Johnston

14 February, 1959

Dear Mama and Dad,

I know you won't get this Valentine for several weeks. I still like to pretend it's like it used to be, when I could make you a Valentine and hand it to you the same day. So pretend that you are here and I can hand you your Valentines like I will to Uncle Jimmy Burr and Uncle George Lee. I gave Mrs. Ruffles one, too. We exchanged them in school. We had to bring a Valentine for everyone in the school. I helped make the Valentine box for us to put them in. It turned out real nice. India Ingrid and Sarah Susan and I worked on it for two days after school. Our teacher said it was one of the prettiest boxes we ever had.

I got some very pretty Valentines, but I got a couple of icky ones, too. There are some of the kids who think I am stuck up or something. I think this is because I say what I think. I never heard of people not wearing a shirt to school, or no socks. As Grandma Alma always says, "You can tell right away what kind of people they are, by the way they dress for church." Well, in this case, it's school, not church. And some of them dress like the junkman did at home.

Uncle Jimmy Burr got mad about that, too. He's in a permanent state of mad with me. I won't tell you what he said about Grandma Alma. All I know is, if she heard him talk, she would say he had "no manners."

Uncle George Lee hasn't said anything about it all. He's kind of quiet about what he thinks. At least he doesn't fly off the handle the way Uncle Jimmy Burr does. That's a new saying I heard here, "fly off the handle." Mrs. Ruffles says it all the time. I go over to her house an awful lot. Especially right after school. She makes treats for India Ingrid and Sarah Susan and I. We especially like her cookies. And Boy! Is her chocolate cake something special. She had just a few pieces of it left the other day, and we ate it in no time. She said she never saw anything like it. She was smiling, though.

I got a Valentine from Judith, too. I sent her one last weekend. I'm glad she got hers on time, too. She wrote me a short letter. Her mother says I can come and visit in the summer and that she can come here and visit, after I go there. Is that all right? I'd like to see my house, even if someone else is renting it for now. Can I please go visit her? Think about it, will you?

Well, I will close now. Oh, by the way, I met a new boy in school. His name is James. He is Doctor MacKenzie's son. That's the doctor who took care of me two weeks ago. Well, he was gone for awhile. No one says anything about where he was, but now he's back. I have heard something about Doctor MacKenzie being divorced and his wife moved away, but that's all I know. Anyway, I met his son, James. He's real nice, but two years older than me. He came into the store the other day and Uncle George Lee introduced me to him. He's going to work after school in the store, being a stock boy. I'd like to do that, too. I'll bet you the Uncles won't let me though. India Ingrid was shocked when I brought it up, but I told her that girls work in Evanston at the movie theaters and grocery stores. Only thing is, you've got to be fifteen and have a work permit. Well, I'm just going to turn fourteen, so that's close. Anyway, why should it matter in Talbotsville? Kids do all kinds of jobs here.

Well, I've got to close now and study. The spelling bee is this coming weekend and I have to be ready for it.

Love and kisses
Amber Lee

28 February, 1959

Dear Moms,

Say hello to Dad, too. Tell him I did get his letter and I will write one especially for him next week. Well, I have a dog! Are you surprised? The Uncles are not in agreement about the dog. One says, "Yes!" One says, "No!" (The "Yes!" won the argument.) Anyway, on the way home from school the other day, I saw this dog get hit by a car. It's just a little dog with blond curls. I don't think it's any special breed 'cause I looked in all my dog books to find one like it. So, I guess it's a mixed breed, as Uncle Jimmy Burr puts it.

Anyway, the car that hit the dog never stopped. The man driving it just yelled at the dog and called it stupid. He didn't even care that it was hurt and bleeding. I saw it happen and got his license plates and reported it to the sheriff. The dog was alive, but it was knocked out. The sheriff was going to shoot it, but I said, "No! Over my dead body!" He said, "Your Uncles aren't going to like this. They got hunting dogs and this one is a cur." Anyhow, I didn't let him shoot it. I asked him to take me to the veterinarian. He laughed at that and said the nearest one was five miles away and he didn't have time to take me there. So I had him take me and the dog to Doctor MacKenzie's office.

The doctor was just leaving to deliver a baby. He told me he didn't do dogs! Meanwhile, this poor little dog was rolling it's eyes and whimpering. Oh, yeah, it was conscious by this time. Oh Mama, you should have seen the look in it's eyes; it would melt a stone.

Well, the doctor left and I thought to myself, I've got to do something. Just then James came home and found me standing there with the dog. He said, "Oh boy! Where did you get that mongrel?" Of course, I told him that this was no mongrel. Anyway, mongrel or not, it was hurt and bleeding and if we didn't do something it would die.

So, he took me into his dad's surgery room. We put the dog on the table and tried to see how bad it was hurt. James got a big basin of soapy water and we scrubbed the wound. There was a real jagged cut on the dogs front right shoulder. So I said, "We are going to have to sew that up." Boy, did he ever look at me. He said he's never sewed a stitch in his life and he wasn't going to start now. So I said, "I'm going to do it. You don't have any experience; I do." Well, Mama, you know when I was working on my Dog and Cat Badge for Girl Scouts, I spent ten hours with the doctor at the animal hospital on Davis Street. He showed me all kinds of things. I even watched surgery on dogs and cats. He told me they don't feel pain like people do, and you can actually stitch up animals without medicine and it doesn't bother them. That's what I told James. He said, never in all his life had he met anyone like me. "Well," I said, "that's too bad, 'cause I'm not a bad sort at all, even if my Uncle Jimmy Burr thinks I'm strange."

Anyway, I did cheat a little,'cause I put some topical anesthetic on the cut. I had to trim the edges a little so it would heal better. I sewed that dog up real quick. It took ten stitches to close the wound. Yes, we really did clean it out good. I even used some hydrogen peroxide to really do a good job. It foamed a lot, like my

12

knee did that time Daddy put it on me to clean a bad cut. Oh, yeah, I forgot to tell you what James did to help. He shaved the hair off the dog, around the cut. He said one time his dad had to stitch his head up, 'cause he cut it open. His dad shaved the hair off around the cut so it would heal better. So we thought we had better do that, too. James knew how to shave better than me 'cause I've never had to do it.

Anyway, we put some salve on it and a big bandage on the wound. Then I took the dog home. You should have heard the commotion about it. Uncle Jimmy Burr could hardly believe that I had sewed up that dog, but he said that anyone who was willing to care that much should be able to keep it! And that was the end of that!

The doctor was another story. He came over that evening to see the dog. He was real mad at James for using his surgery. He said it was for people, not dogs. He even asked James if he should change the sign out front to say: "People *and* Dog Hospital." Actually, I don't think he was as mad as he sounded because I watched him check the dog and then he gave me a real funny look. He asked where I learned to stitch like that. So I told him that I used my best embroidery stitches to do the job. He was very solemn about his inspection and recommended that I be able to keep the dog.

After I left the room, I heard him comment, "If that don't beat all!" And then he started to laugh. I don't mean a quiet laugh either. He laughed for a long time and then told Uncle George Lee that he thought this called for a brandy. I guess they each had a glass and the next thing I heard was all of them laughing. I still don't know what was so funny.

The dog is sleeping in my room with me. Mrs. Ruffles made up a dog bed for her by the side of my bed. I named her 'Caramel' 'cause that's what color she is.

I miss you and love you a lot,

> Your loving daughter,
> Amber Lee Johnston

10 March, 1959

Dear Dad,

I got a job! You'll never guess where in a million years, so I'll tell you—at the doctor's office. He said since I did such a good job on the dog, I could help him in the office on Saturdays. He's teaching me how to clean instruments and sterilize them and I help him clean the office between visits. He has two examination rooms, and while he is using one I clean the other. He had someone who used to have this job, but she moved away after she got married last week. So he needed someone to help and thought of me. He said, I am really awfully young, but given the fact that I was so good at sewing people up (his joke), maybe I could be some help to him in the surgery. Well, we'll see how it all turns out.

How are you, Dad? I haven't had a letter since the first one you sent in January. I know you are busy. I still don't understand why you had to go to Jerusalem for over a year; it's such a long time. Why can't I come over there, too? I don't understand why kids can't go. It doesn't seem fair to me.

And by the way, tell Mom I took second in the spelling bee. It was another one of those small words that did me in. This time it was *moot*! Oh Boy! I was upset. And the person who won is really being a pain in the neck bragging about it. Oh well, at least she doesn't know how to sew up dogs like I do. I guess the whole town is talking about it now. The doctor has told everyone about it. People look at me on the street, but at least now they are talking to me. In the beginning no one noticed me. I even met the blacksmith the other day. Boy, in Evanston you would never have seen a blacksmith. Anyway, he stopped and asked me how the little dog was doing and he petted her. He said it was terrible how some people would hurt animals and leave them to die. He's nice. His name is Merton Crumbie. He's invited me over to meet his sister. He says she is bedridden and cannot go out for walks and meet people. I told him I would be happy to do that next week. So we set up a time and I am going to have tea with Miss Crumbie. I asked him why she was bedridden, but he just looked funny about it, so I decided I had better not be too nosy.

The Uncles agreed with that decision. They were shocked when I told them I was invited for tea. They were not sure they should let me go, but then Mrs. Ruffles assured them I would be okay. I wonder what the fuss is all about. You would think being invited to tea was something unusual in Talbotsville. It's a common, everyday occurrence; except with most people it's coffee—not tea.

Well, I've got to go and do my homework. Please write me more letters. You've only sent one so far.

Love and Kisses,
Amber Lee

15 March, 1959

Dear Mother,

Good grief! How could you even ask such a question! Of course I am attending church! You don't think the Uncles are heathen, do you? They would be shocked. No, I haven't said anything much about it, because it has been an uneventful experience. Now I don't mean boring, just not exactly exciting.

I had dinner at the minister's house about a month ago. Yes, that is unusual, but there were circumstances that led up to it. I went to talk to Reverend Buckley about Confirmation. He wasn't going to let me into the class. He thought I should be held back a year and start in the fall. I said I had been going to classes for one and a half years, and I should be able to be confirmed this year. So, a month ago I went over to the parsonage and decided to beard the lion in his den. (I overheard the Uncles talking about the minister roaring like a lion, so I did kind of have a picture of what his behavior was like.) He was nothing like I had been led to suspect. He told me that since he had not been in charge of my classwork for confirmation, he really couldn't rightly judge how much I knew. So I told him to give me an examination and test my knowledge. I told him I had a letter from our minister in Evanston, but he didn't seem to think too much of that. He said sometimes letters didn't tell the whole story and often that wasn't good enough. This is when I suggested an examination. I asked him to quiz me on anything: The Lord's Prayer and the Petitions, The Creed and the Articles, Bible passages, Bible stories; I told him to even ask me what I believed. Was he surprised, but he did it. I had to go over to his house the next day and take a test that he had invented. Wow! It was something! It is a good thing that I *do* know my stuff. I only missed one question on the whole thing. So, he passed me and said I could come into the class mid-year.

I stayed for dinner, too. He said since I had taken so long over the examination, maybe I needed some refreshment before I went home. His wife is a nice lady, but she can't cook worth a hoot. (These are his words, not mine!) So they have her sister living with them and she does the cooking and manages the household. His wife's name is Genevieve. Her sister's name is Jennifer. I like those names a lot; they sound so romantic. Anyway, dinner was something else. The minister has three children, and Jennifer—she's a widow—has two. There were nine of us at the table. It was a crowd, I can tell you. Reverend Buckley kept trying to stump me on Bible passages, but I really know them pretty good. He says I must have really studied my lessons well. I told him I had.

Well, the final outcome is that I am being confirmed this spring with the rest of his class. Of course, he still tries to trip me up on my Bible passages. But now I'm prepared for him. One of my classmates is his niece and she knows her lessons, too. We are the smartest kids in the class. Even India Ingrid doesn't know hers as well.

Anyway, I just wanted you both to know I am not a heathen yet, and neither are the Uncles.

I enjoyed your last letter a lot. It sounds so interesting there. Can't I come and stay with you this summer? Just think of all the Bible stuff I could learn in Jerusalem. Won't you please think about it before you say no.

Love,
your daughter,
Amber Lee Johnston

28 March, 1959

Dearest Mother,

Oh Boy! I went mushroom picking this morning. Uncle Jimmy Burr says I am a natural. I stumbled over the biggest colony they have ever found. I'm very proud of myself, but Uncle George Lee says not to get too cocky about it. Anyway, the mushrooming was great fun, but the rest of it, ugh! Mrs. Ruffles canned them in little glass pint jars. She says they are a great delicacy and I will be very happy to eat these, come next winter. I think, in a pig's eye! I have absolutely no intention of eating canned mushrooms and I don't care who knows it.

Merton Crumbie laughed about it when I told him what I thought. He said usually little girls weren't too keen on mushrooms anyway. He's really nice. So is his sister. I went there for tea this afternoon and met her for the first time. I am impressed. She is very intelligent and was a teacher for a long time. India Ingrid told me some about her. She says that Miss Crumbie was jilted in love, or something like that. What does that mean, *jilted* in love?

We talked all afternoon. She told me that she had been to Jerusalem and had stayed there for three years. I think that was when she fell in love, but of course I didn't dare ask her about it. Anyway, we talked a lot about books we have both read, and then I told her about sewing up the dog. She asked me specifically about that 'cause her brother Merton had told her about it. She asked me where I learned to sew up dogs. I had to tell her that I taught myself when James and I did it. She said she thought I was awful brave. I told her I really wasn't. Anyway, it was the dog that was brave 'cause she never made a whimper the whole time I was sewing her up. Miss Crumbie wants to meet Caramel. She's very impressed with a dog that is so brave. I said I would bring her over to visit next time I came. We set the date then and there. Miss Crumbie says she likes company and wants to see me regular, so we agreed on me visiting every Tuesday afternoon, right after school.

Well, you should have seen how the Uncles responded to that plan. They talked about Miss Crumbie being very delicate, and that she tired easily, and she sometimes was a little different, and so on. I'm not exactly sure what it is they are not telling me, but I'm sure there is something.

Well, I miss you a lot, both of you. I still don't exactly understand why I can't be there with you, but I'm beginning to find a couple of interesting people down here in Talbotsville.

Love,
Amber Lee

10 April, 1959

Dear Mom and Dad,

I have been very busy the last few weeks. In school we are getting ready for the May Festival. It is an open house at the school so the families of the students can see what kind of work they have been doing all school year. We make up portfolios of our best work and display it. Actually, anyone can look at them, so I really want to do my very best. I want you to be proud of me.

I'm way ahead in reading. Actually, I am reading special assignments because I have already finished the reader they are using in eighth grade in Talbotsville. Our teacher gave me a list of books and I have been meeting with her to discuss them. Secretly, I have been talking about them with Miss Crumbie, too. She is a very good teacher. We have talked about everything I am doing in school and she is afraid that I will get bored. I told her I didn't think there would be any chance of that 'cause there are lots of things in school that keep me interested. The kids more than anything else keep me from being bored. There are all kinds of personalities and you never can tell what will happen next.

I'm also learning a lot more about my friends, India Ingrid and Sarah Susan. India really was named after a character in a book: India Wilkes in *Gone With the Wind*. I thought so, too. I mean, how many people have you ever met named India?

Sarah Susan is interesting, too. She's got a serious health problem. She's got a weak chest, that's what Uncle George Lee told me. He says that's why she can't go out running around with me and India Ingrid in the woods. He says she would get all worn out, and then she could end up in the hospital. I asked, " What is the problem?", but he was real evasive. (Evasive is one of the new words I just learned.) The Uncles are both very good at being evasive. I'll just have to wait it out; sooner or later they will talk to me about it.

My job is coming along real good, too. Doctor MacKenzie keeps me busy on Saturdays. I have to be to the office by 10:30 A.M. He is only there from 11 A.M. until 3 P.M. It's like a half day. There usually is a big crowd, though. You'd think we would never get done in four hours, but we do. I'm very busy cleaning the rooms between visits and sterilizing instruments. But once in a while Doctor MacKenzie has me come in to observe. The patients think it's real interesting to have a girl who assists the doctor.

I have been learning a lot there, too. One of the things I found out is what is wrong with Sarah Susan. She has TB; Tuberculosis is the proper name. I'm sorry I found out, but I guess that is one of the problems of being a doctor, or, as in my case, working for a doctor. You find out things that you don't always want to know. I can't even tell the Uncles what I found out 'cause it's a sacred trust. Doctors take this oath not to tell on people. You know, their diseases and secrets. So, of course I can't tell the Uncles that I really and truly do know what is wrong with Sarah Susan. It scares me. I never knew anyone who was sick before, at least not sick enough to die. I don't even like to think about it. I'm going to have to talk to Doctor MacKenzie and find out the whole truth. Anything would be better than not knowing what is going to happen.

At home we are all finished with the canning of mushrooms. I can tell you, I'm not one bit sorry. We have canned them in brine, and we have canned them in pickling juice, but it doesn't matter to me how we can them; I do not plan on eating any. Mrs. Ruffles says, "Pooh! You'll change your mind. Wait and see." Oh boy! I am not going to change my mind.

I've been cooking other things though. Mrs. Ruffles has taught me how to make *the* chocolate cake. Now I'm the only other person who knows how to make it. I can't even tell you the secret 'cause Mrs. Ruffles made me swear not to tell. (I know what the minister would say about me taking an oath, but believe me, if you ate this cake you'd think it was worth it too.) Anyway, I made it the other day for the first time and it turned out great. I served it to the Uncles and to India Ingrid and Sarah Susan. All of them thought Mrs. Ruffles made it. I didn't tell them the truth, but I felt I had done a good job baking it. That's a relief to know 'cause the recipe is not written down; it's all in my head and I will never forget it.

I took a small wedge of it to Miss Crumbie and Mr. Merton Crumbie. I like him real fine. He is a handsome man and I wonder why he is not married. I asked Miss Crumbie about it, but she just said that he never seemed interested in anyone enough to marry them. "Well," I told her, "I think that is a real shame!" She liked the cake a lot, so did Merton. I've decided if either one of them ever decides to get married I will give them the chocolate cake recipe, with a little variation. That way I won't really be giving away Mrs. Ruffles secret recipe.

Well, I'd better close now. I sure am getting long winded lately. Uncle Jimmy Burr told me recently the way I gab, it's like somebody put in a nickel and they're getting a dollars worth. I asked him if he thought I talk too much, but he said, "No." So I don't know what to think. I do know this though: I'm beginning to mutter under my breath, just like Uncle Jimmy Burr. I don't know if that's a good sign or not. Uncle George Lee doesn't think so. He says the next thing I'll begin to look like Uncle Jimmy Burr and then I'll be in serious trouble. I just laughed at that.

Write to me soon.

Love,
Amber Lee

25 April, 1959

Dear Mom,

I've just come home from dinner at India Ingrid's house. Her mother let us play in the attic and we found all sorts of things up there. One of your old yearbooks was there and so the two of us spent all evening looking at it. It is so surprising; I look just like you did when you were young. We could be sisters. India Ingrid's mother agreed wholeheartedly. She says that I am the spitting image of you and sometimes when she sees me, it is like stepping back in time.

Sarah Susan and I tried on dress-up clothes from old trunks, too. Sarah Susan tried on one dress that was from Paris, France. She says she would sure like to have a dress from Paris for herself sometime. She says it's her dire wish to have a Paris fashion to wear before she dies. It gave me the chills in my spine when she said that, and I just couldn't get over it. Oh, Mama, I've got this most terrible feeling about Sarah Susan. I've been reading Doctor MacKenzie's medical books about diseases and it says TB is fatal, unless people go to dry climates and rest a lot. It's damp here, just like Chicago. Her family doesn't have any money to send her to a warm, dry climate. Does this mean she's going to die? People shouldn't have to die until they get real old, should they?

Send me a letter real soon with some pictures. I want to see what it looks like there. Is it warm? I suppose it is just the kind of climate Sarah Susan needs. All my geography books talk about the arid climate of Palestine. When are you coming home? You haven't said anything about that yet.

Oh, and thanks for saying I can go and visit in Evanston. Judith will be thrilled when I tell her the news. The Uncles said she can come and visit here for two weeks, too. We will be able to spend four weeks together. I can hardly wait until school lets out in June.

The May Festival is coming along real well. I have one of the lead parts in the operetta we are putting on for the parents and friends. I have been practicing my lines with Uncle George Lee. He sort of fancies himself as an actor, so we have been having a good time practicing.

Easter was wonderful. Doctor MacKenzie gave me another pet—actually six pets. He gave me a half dozen hens to raise by myself. He says it will keep me out of mischief after school lets out for the summer. He says chores are what build character, and all kids—especially girls—need things to keep them occupied. I told him I felt I was doing just fine without any more responsibility heaped on me. After all, I work for him on Saturdays. He did agree that while I was in Evanston he would consider that vacation time. But when I came home, friend visiting or not, I had a job every Saturday all summer. I guess she will find things to keep her occupied while I am busy. He drives a tough bargain.

Confirmation will be in the fall. Reverend Buckley says he likes to wait until after summer is over, and he can see how much we remember of our lessons. He says it separates the wheat and the chaff, whatever that means. Anyway, it has been a very busy time. We are also just finishing up with our spring cleaning. This really is a big event. I offered to help 'cause I thought I could talk the Uncles into letting me clean the attic. (I love attics.) They said, "No dice." Uncle George Lee said that cleaning the attic would disturb it's "atmosphere." Well, I don't know anything about that; it certainly would clean up some of those unsavory mouse nests Mrs. Ruffles talks about. The Uncles wouldn't have any of it though, no matter how much I pleaded. So, I finally gave up on the idea and helped downstairs. We even polished all the silverware.

It was while we were doing this that Mrs. Ruffles told me how you ran away from home to marry daddy. Well, actually she didn't offer the information right out; she slipped and said something about it and I heard it. So I kept asking and pestering until she told me. She said not to tell the Uncles; they would be mad at her. No wonder you never said anything about the Talbots. Mrs. Ruffles thinks it was awful how my grandfather carried on about it. She said he raved for years and it was probably the reason for his early demise. (I don't know about that; Doctor MacKenzie said he died of an accident in the car.) Anyway, I have now heard the whole story. Mrs. Ruffles prides herself on her ability to be objective about things and not be opinionated. I'm not so sure about that 'cause she keeps referring to my grandfather as a "stubborn old mule of an old man."

Now that I have heard the true story, maybe you'll tell me about how you eloped. It sounds so romantic. I want to know if you climbed down a ladder at midnight.

Write to me soon and tell me the answers. Oh, by the way, have you gotten over the flu yet? It sounds bad to me. Doctor MacKenzie says you should be sure to drink enough fluids and take aspirin. He said if you weren't off traipsing all over the Middle East, you probably wouldn't be sick.

The Uncles say hello!

Love,
Amber Lee

5 May, 1959

MAMA!

What do you mean, I'm going to have a sister or brother? Good grief! I don't know whether to laugh or to cry. The Uncles don't know which to do either. It is the talk of the household, as well as the town. You don't really think Mrs. Ruffles can keep a secret like this, do you? Oh, Mama, remember how much we talked about babies and maybe we could get one, and now you are in Jerusalem and you're going to get one. The Uncles are wondering if you will come home to have the baby, but I can already guess the answer to that question. No! Babies are born in Jerusalem, too. After all, the baby Jesus was born over there, so you'll agree that it must be okay. Just don't name him some biblical name that's real long and no one can pronounce it. Uncle George Lee thinks you should name him Hezekiah or Jephthah. (I have a suspicion he has been pouring over names in the Bible to find something odd.) I told him you didn't need any help and probably had names picked out already.

The weather has turned absolutely fine. Spring is so wonderful here. Of course, I love it in Evanston, too. I really miss Lake Michigan a lot. Judith and I used to go down to the lake and just watch the waves come in for hours. The lake here is nothing like that and you can see to the other side of it.

There is a place in the woods (near where I found the mushrooms), where the violets are so thick they are like a carpet. I call it The Fairies' Parlor. It is way back in among the thickest trees you have ever seen. It looks like no one ever comes here at all. So Caramel and I come here to sit and read our lessons. I have been working on my lines for the play (Uncle George Lee is surprised on how well I know them), and I have been busy writing a story. The story is a surprise for the May Festival. I will tell you all about it when I am done.

I have also been meeting new people. There is a little farm out here on the way to the woods. I saw the farmer out planting one day and he invited me in to meet his wife. She gave me tea and a glass of fresh milk. It doesn't seem to matter whether or not you drink the tea, it's more a formality.

I always drink the tea, too. I think it's good practice to mind my manners and eat what people give me. At prayers every evening the Uncles talk a lot about the needs of people; I'm beginning to understand what they are talking about in Talbotsville.

Anyway, the farmer's name is Fenwick, Deuteronomy Fenwick! (Now I am convinced we don't want any biblical names.) He said he went to school with you and the Uncles. He found an old album, and there you were. It's a wonderful picture of you and the Uncles out picking berries right near here. In fact, he said it's not far from The Fairies' Parlor. So, of course I had to look for the spot. I found it, too. I think there must be zillions of berry bushes there. I am going to come back here with India Ingrid, Sarah Susan, and Judith, when she visits.

Oh, yes, and before I forget, we had a wonderful cake for tea. Mr. Fenwick's wife can cook, unlike Reverend Buckley's wife, who is a cousin. It was an angel food, hand beaten. I had this vision of Mrs. Fenwick beating eggs all day just to make this cake. She also had lemon cream pie. She says they always go together 'cause you have so many yolks left over from the beaten egg whites, and it's nice to make something special with them, too. She's a very nice lady. I really like her a lot. She told me she has all sorts of special places in the woods and goes there as often as she can. We have a lot in common. I never thought grown-ups could be so much fun to talk to, but they are.

Miss Crumbie is looking ever so much better. Mr. Merton Crumbie says it's 'cause she has something to look forward to every week. Last week Uncle George Lee took me over there 'cause it was raining. He came in and had tea, too. I didn't know he knew Miss Crumbie so well. He called her by her first name, which is Griselda. I still call her by her formal name, though; I know my manners, Mama.

On the way home Uncle George Lee made a comment about what a shame it is that Griselda is an invalid. When I asked him what happened, he said no one really knew what was wrong. She just got up one day and had difficulty walking. I think that is a terrible shame, too.

Well, I am going to do my lessons and work on my writing. Please write me and assure me that you will not find any funny Bible names for my brother.

Love and Kisses,
Amber Lee

12 May, 1959

Dear Mom and Dad,
    Once again I'm in a little trouble. Well, actually, there are several

things that happened. One is bad; one is good; and one is real good! The real good makes up for the bad.

It's Miller's Pond again. I really think I will need to stay as far away from that place as I can. There is no point in beating around the bush, so I will tell you quick! I fell in, again! I was totally drenched in my good Sunday outfit and the Uncles are really mad at me this time.

Now, I will tell you the real good news! When I fell in the pond Mr. Merton Crumbie and his sister, Miss Griselda Crumbie, were driving past on the way home from church. They saw me fall off the fishing dock and into the pond. In a flash Miss Crumbie was out of that car and ran as fast as she could. She dove into the lake and saved me. I didn't have the heart to tell her that I was a very good swimmer (you had to be to swim in Lake Michigan), and that I could have saved myself. The long and the short of it is, Miss Crumbie is walking again. Of course, Mr. Merton Crumbie took her to Doctor MacKenzie to be examined, but she's as good as new.

Now, not only am I known as the "Girl Who Sews up Dogs," but I am also "The Girl Who Causes Invalids to Walk!"

So, that brings me to the last piece of news. I wrote a story called "The Girl Who Sews Up Dogs" and sold it to the local newspaper. It will be printed in time for the May Festival and will be on sale at the school. The proceeds will be used to buy some new books for the classrooms. I got so tired of people asking me about Caramel and what happened that I decided to write about it. At least it may cut down on the asking if I tell them to read my story.

All of this happened several days ago. Now I need to tell you what's going on as a result of all this activity. Uncle George Lee is sweet on Miss Crumbie! Oh, yes, he is! You should see him. He goes over to check on her every day, and Uncle Jimmy Burr talks about it all the time. Says he was "head over ears" years ago and that nothing has changed. Well, I think he's wrong that nothing has changed. It sounds like years ago Miss Crumbie was not sweet on Uncle George Lee, but now she sure as shooting is. She's as glad to see him every day as he is to see her. Uncle Jimmy Burr says, "Mark my words, there's going to be a wedding here yet!" I think he's right, Mama; Uncle George Lee is going to get married. Do you think she'll come here to live with us? That's what Uncle Jimmy Burr says. He keeps talking about what a big house this is, and it needs the sound of children laughing in it. I suppose that's why they like it when India Ingrid and Sarah Susan come over here. We laugh all the time. Mrs. Ruffles feeds us treats every day after school and then we sit on the side porch and do our homework and projects. It's getting nice and warm all the time now. Spring is really here. Next weekend is the school picnic over by Miller's Pond. (I know what you're thinking, so, yes! I will behave myself!)

I know my part for the play. Uncle George Lee says I am letter perfect. The book is all printed and ready to pick up at the newspaper office. And all of my schoolwork is ready to be displayed for the May Festival. There is a pot luck supper that night and a rummage and craft sale. It's so exciting that we can hardly wait. Mrs. Ruffles says she just can't understand what all the fuss is about; one May Festival is just like another! I don't think that's true at all.

Well, I will be sure to keep you informed about the romance. It's so exciting! I don't dare think about it too much or I would never get any sleep at night.

Love for now,
Amber Lee Johnston

31 May, 1959

Dearest Mommy,

What a week! Thank goodness it's all behind us now. There have been so many things happening that I don't know where to begin!

First, Uncle George Lee did propose. Second, she accepted the proposal. The wedding is planned for this September. Uncle Jimmy Burr says, "Hurrah!" Mrs. Ruffles says, "Indecent haste!" I say, "Oh, Boy! Miss Griselda Crumbie is going to be my Aunt! Could anything be more wonderful!?"

The whole town is talking about us! But it's good talk. I'm beginning to understand more fully about bad talk. There's some of that going around, too.

The Latimer twins set fire to Mrs. Polk's barn. Now everyone is saying how bad these boys have always been and what else could you expect? The Uncles say it is a shame how everyone is talking about the twins. But who offered to help when Mrs. Latimer died two years ago and Mr. Latimer asked for help to manage them? They've always been a handful, but never malicious (that's the Uncles word). I like the twins. They are two years behind me in school and are really very smart. I think they get bored; that's half the problem. But then, I'm just an eighth grader, so what I think doesn't count much anyhow.

When it comes down to it, there wasn't that much damage to the barn. The boys called for help the minute they saw how bad it was, so really it could have been much worse.

The Uncles are putting them to work at the store, as stock boys. They say it will keep them out of mischief during the summer, and next fall they'll see what else to do with them. Of course, this absolutely means that I can't work at the store; they don't have any more jobs for anyone else. The Uncles are shocked that I am considering such an idea, but I tell them I have some monetary needs, too.

Miss Crumbie is going to live here, so the Uncles have hired the town handyman, Jerald Crisp, to redecorate the whole house. Oh dear, this is going to be a long project. Of course, there is no major structural work (the Uncles words), but the walls have gotten shocking dirty (Mrs. Ruffles words). So every room, closet, and pantry, from basement to attic will be painted and papered. Miss Crumbie is already sitting down with Mr. Crisp to get it all organized. Even my room is going to be done and Miss Crumbie has picked out new wallpaper and fabric for the curtains and bedspread. It's so exciting!

It's not going to be hard to call Miss Crumbie, "Aunt Griselda" either. I catch myself saying it already. She is really wonderful. I know you are going to love her as much as I do. She is a couple of years older than you, but that's not so much.

The May Festival was absolutely the most wonderful time. All of my schoolwork had A's and my book, "The Girl Who Sews Up Dogs" did a brisk business. There was enough money made to buy some new books for the school library and a little left over for something else. The play was a lot of fun and we had a standing ovation. I think in a town this size, that's a real success! Remember *South Pacific* in Chicago? How thrilled I was? Well, this was just as good! I'm not exaggerating; we really were that good!

The pot luck supper was such fun. I don't think I have ever been to one before this. How come we never go to these kind of things in Evanston? They must have them there, too. The Uncles say Lutherans have them all the time. Uncle Jimmy Burr says it isn't a true Lutheran Church if there aren't any pot luck suppers. Does this mean our church isn't up to snuff? (This is you know who's quote.) Anyway, you can bet I will notice in the future what we do at church in Evanston.

I will be graduating from eighth grade next month. The Uncles and Aunt Griselda are planning a graduation party for me. They have Mr. Crisp doing the downstairs decorating first. This way, Uncle George Lee says, "The townsfolk won't think our walls are 'shocking dirty!'" Mrs. Ruffles isn't saying anything more. Secretly, I agree with her. She says nothing has been done since you left home. She says if Grandma had been alive, it would have been different. But as it was, all that's ever been done is spring and fall cleaning and some wall washing in the bad spots.

My job is going great! Doctor MacKenzie let me go on house calls with him the other day. That was real interesting, too. He quizzes me on what I think is the matter with people and I tell him. I have met a lot more people with TB. He says it is very prevalent, especially where people work in the mines. That's where Sarah Susan's father works, and he has TB, too. Doctor MacKenzie says people also get some kind of lung disease from working in the mines, too. I don't know much about that!

I have met a lot of new people when I go with the doctor. He knows everyone in the county, I think. There is one little old man who has invited me to come and visit him again. He is a wood carver and he has the most wonderful carvings. He creates sprites, and fairies, and wood gnomes, as well as animals and people. It's just wonderful to look at all of his creations. I told Doctor MacKenzie I would never have any money at all if I bought all of them that I liked.

You haven't said yet when I am going to get a new brother. The Uncles have asked me to ask you and Dad. So, when will the baby be born? Please let us know as soon as possible so we can plan something, like a shower in absentia. (That word I learned from Doctor MacKenzie.)

The school picnic was a great success. I did not fall in Miller's Pond, although there were some questionable moments when I was tempted to walk the railroad bridge. All of the other kids did it, but I withstood and was firm about resisting. I know what the Uncles would have said if I had fallen in again.

Well, that's about all I have to say, other than I love you and miss you both.

Amber Lee

❦

15 June, 1959

Dear Mom and Dad,

I am all graduated. Thank you for the wonderful present from Jerusalem. I was at the top of my class. I don't know how important this is, as there were only four of us. It doesn't seem like too much of a distinction to me. The Uncles were thrilled and said they expected as much, seeing as how I love to read and am so knowledgeable about things. I wore the dress for my graduation and had a lot of compliments on it. I said it was from the Holy Land and it was from my parents. Aunt Griselda says the color is just right for my complexion and it brings out the sheen of my hair. She fixed my hair in a pageboy for graduation. It really looked nice. I guess I'm all done with braids and Uncle George Lee helping plait my hair every morning. I will admit he did a good job, but now I have to have a more grown-up hairdo.

The downstairs is all decorated, at least the things that needed to be painted. The wall papering and the rest of the house will be done while I am gone to Evanston. I will be leaving at the end of this week. It doesn't seem possible that school is out already. Uncle Jimmy Burr says, "Time flies faster when you are a grown-up." And I believe him, too.

Sarah Sue and India Ingrid are saying they miss me already and I'm not even gone yet. I told them that I will miss them a lot and that they are also my best friends, so they shouldn't worry about Judith taking all my affection. I said we were blood sisters—we had this ceremony like the Indians do—and that nothing will ever interfere in our friendship. I don't know whether they believe me or not, but they should. I will only be gone for two weeks. Even Doctor MacKenzie says it will be hard to fill my shoes while I am gone to Evanston. I told him he shouldn't be so dependent on my help. What if I got sick or something? He needs to have a substitute for these dire occasions.

India Ingrid is going to take care of my hens for me while I am gone and she said she will be sure and take Caramel for long walks in the woods. I know it will be hard to explain to a dog why I have to go away for two weeks, but I am trying hard to tell her. She just looks at me with that look that "tugs your heart stings" and whimpers a little. I bet she knows something is in the wind. Is this how I looked when you and Dad left for Jerusalem? Oh boy, that must have been terrible hard to go and leave me. After this year is over I don't think any of us will want to go away again for a long time. I try very hard not to think about how Caramel feels about it. India Ingrid says, "That dog is not human; you've got to stop worrying about her feelings, Amber Lee!"

I guess she is right. Well, next week at this time I will be in Evanston. I will write to you when I get there.

Love and Kisses,
Amber Lee

22 June, 1959

Dear Mama,

Well, I am here. The train ride was a little scary as we derailed on a curve. The porter said the engineer was speeding. The engineer said he had to "throw on the brakes." The railroad said its good no one got hurt! Well, I guess that's true in a way. I don't think anyone was real seriously hurt, but there were some people burned in the dining car. There was scalding water and some of the people had it spilled on them. Those were the only injuries though. I am fine. I thought I had better write and tell you about it before Uncle Jimmy Burr sends one of his infamous telegrams to you. At least this time it's not because I fell in a pond, or caught Pneumonia. This time it's to let you know I am safe and sound at home in Evanston.

Well, Mother, I never thought you would hear me say this, but sometimes I think Judith acts like a child! I have been here three days and I'm wondering if I really want to stay for the whole two weeks. For one thing, I miss the Uncles and Mrs. Ruffles and Aunt Griselda. For another, I miss India Ingrid and Sarah Susan and Caramel. But for a third thing, Judith is all besotted with a boy who works at Walker Bros. Restaurant as a busboy and all she wants to do is to drink Cokes and eat french fries and look at him. It's disgusting. She keeps telling me I've become a country bumpkin. Says I don't know what it is to be in love 'cause I'm too countrified. I'm not sure what she means by all that, but I do feel quite insulted. She acts as if people in the country don't know anything, as if we're all kind of backward. I told her she better not be talking out of turn 'cause I graduated at the top of my class, and where did she rank in her class? That shut her up for awhile. I suppose I'm sounding kind of mean about all this, but it really agitates me.

Another thing, we were going to spend a lot of time at the lake and go swimming, and go to Harms Woods and go horseback riding, and we haven't done any of that. Judith says she is getting too grown up to go to the beach and lie there like a sausage on a spit. She says, "I have to be careful of my complexion. Too much sun isn't good for you." I think what happened is she saw *Gone With the Wind* too many times and thinks she is Scarlet O'Hara. Honestly, Mother, I don't know about this; maybe I should just go back home to Talbotsville. Doctor MacKenzie would be happy to see me and I know the Uncles would be thrilled to have me home. But I think it might be bad manners to just say I want to leave, so I suppose I will just have to grin and bear it for two weeks.

I went by our house and visited with the people who are renting it. They seem very nice. They have three children and a dog and a cat. It seems funny to have animals in our house, but they are taking good care of the furniture. Of course, I really couldn't inspect too close 'cause they had slip covers on everything. Mrs. Ruffles says people use slip covers to cover a multitude of sins. How can furniture have sins?

Speaking of sins, I am going to church this Sunday. Judith's mother said she will take me there and pick me up after the service. They are Catholic and dare not go into a Lutheran Church or else. I'm not sure what the "or else" means. Judith doesn't seem to know and her mother kind of ignores me when I ask.

Oh yes, Judith's other favorite place to go is Cooley's Cupboard. It's a high school hangout and she wants to get a head start on doing what is expected. We have been downtown Evanston and it is wonderful to be back here. I really love it here. I like the lake so much. I don't think I will ever be able to live anywhere else, but here. Don't you miss it, too?

Well, I'd better close now. Judith is pestering to go to Walker Bros. Restaurant again. I'm going to hate those hamburgers and skinny little french fries. I will write again soon.

Love,
Amber Lee

26 June 1959

Dear Mother,

Oh, I don't know where to start. It has been better the last four days. For one thing, I ran into some of my other friends here and we all went out to Harms Woods for a picnic and went horseback riding. My favorite horse, Jack, is still there and the owner says he has missed me. Of course, I spoiled that horse rotten to the bone most every time I rode him. It wouldn't surprise me one bit if he really did miss me. Though I don't think horses have such good memories. I know dogs do, so I worry about Caramel. Anyway, we had a perfectly marvelous time out at the woods. When I got home Judith was moping around like an old wet hen. She says I am here visiting her, so why am I going all these places without her? Honestly, Mama, how can she have gotten so drippy in six months? I told her she was my dearest friend in all the world and she did not have to worry if I did things with someone else. That seemed to make her feel better, especially after I said I would go to Walker Bros. with her this evening. Oh, I am so sick of little french fries! I think I'll have ice cream.

The other thing is, I went to supper at our minister's house. I told him and his wife all about Talbotsville and how Reverend

Buckley confirms people in the fall, instead of in the spring. I said it's to "separate the wheat from the chaff," according to Reverend Buckley. Pastor Rathbone said that notion had never occurred to him, but that Reverend Buckley might just have a good idea there.

Pastor Rathbone listened intently when I told him about what the Uncles had said about pot luck suppers being a Lutheran institution. He said we have them, but not nearly so often as it sounds like we do in Talbotsville. He promised he would look into the situation at Bethany, 'cause he didn't think we wanted to be less Lutheran than our country friends. He looked so serious, I thought I had made one of those social blunders you worry about so much, but then I noticed the twinkle in his eye.

We had a very nice visit. Of course, my class here is all confirmed already. In some ways I feel left out, but on the other hand, Reverend Buckley is such a challenge to impress that it's almost fun.

Judith went to church with me and commented that it seemed very civilized and all that! Really, Mother, what do you think she really thinks about our religion? Someday, you know, all this silly stuff between Catholics and Lutherans will end. I just don't understand what the fuss is all about. One of Dad's cousins married a Catholic and she seems like the same person and still believes in Jesus. Oh well, I don't think there's anything I can do about it, so I might as well not worry.

We sat up and talked like the old days when I lived here, except that now all she wants to talk about is Bobby Vickers. He's the busboy at Walker Bros. I have to admit he is kind of cute, but I still don't understand why that's all she wants to talk about. And I know if I admit to her that I think he is cute, my fish is fried. (That is one of Uncle Jimmy Burr's favorite sayings, when he knows he's in for it from Mrs. Ruffles.) Oh well, we are going to go to Chicago tomorrow to the Museum. I think finally Judith has decided we need to do some sightseeing while I am here. Her mother is probably behind this idea.

When Judith comes back to Talbotsville with me, we are going to spend a day at Starved Rock State Park. She's all excited about that 'cause Bobby said he was there last year and he really thought it was "neat." At least we are talking more and arguing less. It's only taken a week to get back on the track.

Well, I will close for now. I did enjoy your last letter an awful lot. I hope you are taking care of yourself and my new brother. (See how sure I am about this!) The Uncles still think you should come home to have the baby and so does Judith's mother. I don't know what I think, but I guess the baby could be born there as well as here.

Write soon.

Love
Amber Lee

5 July, 1959

Dear Mom and Dad,

We have been having a wonderful time. Yesterday we went on a picnic and to the parade on Davis Street. Then we went to Dyche Stadium for the fireworks. It almost seemed as if the day would never end. Not in a bad way, though; it was really wonderful! Sometimes it happens that a day is so perfect, it's almost *too* perfect. It seemed like my heart would break from happiness. There was only one thing wrong; you and Daddy weren't here.

Oh, sometimes I miss you so much; I don't think I can stand it anymore. That's what I'm talking about exactly: You're so happy you can't stand it, yet you're so unhappy you can't stand it either. How can a person feel two exactly opposite things like that at the same time? It's a real puzzler. (Uncle George Lee's favorite saying.)

I think I miss the Uncles, too. And I miss the sound of Mrs. Ruffles yelling up the stairs, "Up! Up! Miss! You'll be late if you don't hurry up and eat your breakfast." Don't ever tell her that I said she yells. Mrs. Ruffles talks all the time about how young ladies should act, but she doesn't always do it herself, especially when it comes to raising her voice. The thing is though, she is so exactly like what you think a little old Scottish lady should be. Her brogue is the same as it has always been, since she came to the United States. That's what the Uncles said. They told me she came to Talbotsville when you were all children, and that the only things that have changed since are her black dresses. Anyway, I miss her a lot.

Next week this time, Judith and I will be in Talbotsville. I'll tell you something secret: I will be very glad to go home! It was nice to visit everyone, but I'm homesick for the Uncles.

I will write again soon.

Love and Kisses,
Amber Lee Johnston

13 July, 1959

Dear Mother,

Well, we are here again! And I am so glad to be home. I missed Caramel so much. She is beside herself with joy to see me. The Uncles are almost like that, too. Of course, Uncle Jimmy Burr

40

would never admit that he missed me, but he is being so courtly that I am greatly suspicious. Aunt Griselda says it has not been the same since I left. I'll say that is the truth! Wait until you see the house! It is almost unbelievable! The wallpaper is all hung and all the rooms are completely painted. The downstairs wasn't finished when I left, but now it is. Oh, Mama, you should see it! Mrs. Ruffles says it hasn't looked so grand since it was built. I must say, it is truly beautiful. I think this is what must be meant by "a woman's touch."

There is no describing what Uncle George Lee is like these days, so I don't know that I will even try. But a clue is, Uncle Jimmy Burr says, "He's so light, he could walk on water." So I guess that's a good description.

Mrs. Ruffles is the same. She gave me all the news in about a half hour, and now we are all settled in. Judith doesn't know quite what to think. She has just been taking it all in and being very quiet.

The train ride was so much better than when I came in January. We had a wonderful time. Judith and I had a sleeper on the train. It was a real experience I can tell you. First, they pull the bed right down out of the wall. That's quite a surprise in itself, but then you lift up this bench and there is your own private bathroom, right in your car. Judith says, "It's superb!" I don't know if I think superb is quite the right description, but it certainly is convenient.

We didn't get a chance to really meet anyone on the train, as we slept through almost the whole trip.

It was fun! The porter was so kind. He came to help us put the bed down and to see what time we wanted to get up in the morning. He said we were too young for morning call coffee, but he thought as how he could bring us some hot chocolate with a marshmallow. He brought us a sweet roll, too. It was caramel with a lot of pecans, just like I like them.

41

Judith said she felt so grown up, tipping the porter, that I didn't say anything about being an old hand at traveling.

She's also raving about Uncle Jimmy Burr. She says his name is so elegant. This is a very nice change from hearing about Bobby Vickers, but I just don't understand it. He seems like the same Uncle Jimmy Burr to me. I will admit, he has been going out of his way to be especially polite to her (with me he's exactly the same as always), but it still doesn't make any sense to me.

Mrs. Ruffles says she is very happy that I am home 'cause now she has someone young and spry to pick peas. Oh, yes, I forgot to tell you about the garden. I think I forgot 'cause I just knew it was going to be a lot of work! Anyway, my first morning home I picked peas for two hours. It seems like there are endless rows of everything, lots of peas. Judith didn't have to help 'cause she's company. What a bother! I wonder how long she will qualify as company. After all, aren't I company, too? Mrs. Ruffles says we have a big garden 'cause we give a lot of it away to people who are not as well off as ourselves. (I still think they could pick their own peas.) It isn't just the picking either. After that is done, then you have to shell the peas. I don't know which is worse! Judith did help with that chore 'cause the reward was cookies and milk. (These were Fairy Slipper cookies, and Judith was properly impressed!) Then, after all that work was done we had to can the peas!

Mother, they put up their own vegetables here. I don't understand why. The Uncles own the General Store and sell groceries, so why do they put up their own food? Mrs. Ruffles tells me it's 'cause home-canned tastes better and is the real thing. I just thought things tasted good 'cause Mrs. Ruffles is the best cook in town. Anyway, I can already see that summer is going to be one long list of chores.

I introduced Judith to Doctor MacKenzie. He showed her around his office and told her about my job. After that he gave us

Cokes and we sat on the front porch to drink them. James came home from the store just then, so we all sat and talked until dark. When James walked us home afterwards I noticed how much taller he had gotten since I first met him. He really is a very nice boy and seems so grown up. I suppose that's from working in the store with the Uncles. Of course, James is in charge of managing the Latimer twins, too. He finds chores for them to do and sends them out on deliveries. Actually, the twins are doing real well and putting their paychecks in the bank. First they have to pay back for the damage to Mrs. Polk's barn, but then they plan to save for college. I think that's wonderful. And even though James doesn't admit it, I'll bet the idea for college came from him.

James plans on going to college and studying law; then he plans to live here. He says, "There's no place like Talbotsville; the people are so nice. There's no place like Talbotsville; the fields and woods are so beautiful." Honestly, he sounds like Dorothy in *The Wizard of Oz!*—"There's no place like home! There's no place like home!" Oh well, I guess it's okay here, I kind of missed it a little when I was in Evanston.

The Uncles and Caramel send their love.

Amber Lee

20 July, 1959

Dear Mother,

I have never been so surprised in all my life. Caramel had babies! I hardly had time to realize it before it happened. Uncle Jimmy Burr said he had suspected as much because the little minx had been making eyes at his hunting dog, Bud. Of course, I couldn't believe it 'cause Bud is as homely as a mud fence and I said so. Why on earth would a pretty dog like Caramel bother with him? Uncle Jimmy Burr just rolled his eyes at Uncle George Lee and said, "You explain it to her; I don't know if I can."

That was one heck of a conversation, I can tell you. Uncle George Lee calls it his "Beauty is in the eye of the beholder" speech instead of "the birds and the bees." It was an interesting half hour of talk. Uncle George Lee did say there were a couple of things he would leave for Aunt Griselda to address. She's coming to dinner later today.

The puppies are gorgeous! Judith says she absolutely is going to have one of these pups. She says they are the darlingest dogs she has ever seen.

Judith has met India Ingrid and Sarah Susan, too. We have all been going out in the woods to picnic, when I'm not picking peas and beans. We get up every morning and go out and do our garden chores. Judith is now helping 'cause she says it makes the work go faster and I have more time to spend with her. Now that I'm getting used to it, it's not so bad. We have a system for picking and cleaning the peas and beans. By the time we take them into the kitchen all that's left for Mrs. Ruffles to do is to put them in jars and pressure cook them. We pick and clean them in the morning and she puts them up all afternoon. She even has the Uncles involved. They work in the garden every day. Uncle Jimmy Burr cultivates and Uncle George Lee hoes. Uncle Jimmy Burr is very careful with the cultivating and does a beautiful job. When Uncle George Lee does it he damages the plants. So he's stuck with the hoe. He gripes a lot about it, too.

The picnics have been going well, too. Every day after working in the garden, Mrs. Ruffles has a picnic lunch put up for us in a wicker hamper. Judith and I go meet India Ingrid and Sarah Susan and then we walk out to The Fairies' Parlor to have our picnic. It's so beautiful there. First we have lunch, and then we take turns reading stories to one another. Now we are reading *Little Women* and it's a lot of fun. We also have picked buckets and buckets of berries. India Ingrid's mother is making jelly from them. There are lots of different kinds, raspberries, blueberries, and currants. My fingers are getting all stained. Judith thinks it's so much fun here that she called her mother and dad last night to ask if she could stay until the middle of August. The Uncles talked on the phone with her parents and said it was a fine idea. So, we are all going to be together for most of the summer. I feel so happy about it. My best friends in all the world are here and we are having such a wonderful time. I have this funny feeling inside that in my whole life there will never again be such a time as this. So I really want to enjoy it a much as I can.

We are going to Starved Rock. Uncle Jimmy Burr and Uncle George Lee have taken a day off for the event. A whole bunch of us are going, Sarah Susan and her mother, India Ingrid and her parents, Aunt Griselda and Mrs. Ruffles, and even Doctor MacKenzie, James, and the Latimer twins. We are going in a caravan of cars. It will be so wonderful. The only bad thing is Sarah Susan cannot climb to the top of Starved Rock and will have to wait for us at the bottom. Her father couldn't go either 'cause he has that lung disease from working in the mines. Still, it will be a *big* event in my life, so I am looking forward to it.

I am back at work, too. Doctor MacKenzie's office has been very busy on Saturdays. Last week we worked five and a half hours, instead of four. I told him that at this rate he will have to raise my pay. He just laughed about that and said we would have to renegotiate our agreement.

Deuteronomy Fenwick's wife was in to see the Doctor. She is going to have a baby and it is supposed to arrive very soon. They are very excited about the baby 'cause they didn't think they could have any. I think it is very wonderful and I am excited about it. Mr. Fenwick has made a baby cradle and a rocking chair for Mrs. Fenwick. They are made out of cherry wood and are beautiful. He even painted tiny flowers and little animals on them. Doctor MacKenzie says that Mr. Fenwick could sell them for a fancy price, if he wanted to.

Well, I will write again soon. I love you both lots.

Amber Lee

23 July, 1959

Dear Mama,

Oh, I don't know where to start! The trip or the baby! Goodness, it has been exciting here! I guess I'll start with the baby!

Mrs. Fenwick had her baby girl! It's so exciting! You see, she is named after me! Edith Amber! Edith is for Mrs. Fenwick's mother, but the Amber is for me. Now for the whole story. I helped deliver the baby!

We were out for our daily picnic at The Fairies' Parlor when I heard someone calling us. So I ran out of the woods and there was Deuteronomy Fenwick looking frantic. He said his phone wasn't working and the baby was coming. He needed Doctor MacKenzie real quick. India Ingrid took off like a shot, running to town. I ran with Mr. Fenwick to the farmhouse. Oh, Mama, it was true! Mrs. Fenwick was going to have her baby right then and there. I told Sarah Susan and Judith to put on a kettle and bring me some sheets and towels. I was so glad I had been there when Caramel had her puppies. I know it's not quite the same, but I had a pretty good idea of what was going to happen. Poor Mr. Fenwick didn't know what to do, but I told him to help me undress Mrs. Fenwick and where to put the towels. There wasn't any more time than that. Just that quick the baby started to be born. Mama, it's so strange; I knew just what I had to do. The baby had its cord wrapped around its neck, so I just slid my finger up inside of it and slid it around the baby's head. It worked ever so slick and nice. Then after the baby was born I held it upside down so any drainage in its throat would come out easier. Then, I gave the baby a couple of spanks on its butt and it started to cry. After that I wrapped it in clean blankets and just let it lay by Mrs. Fenwick. That's when Doctor MacKenzie got there and took over. It was a lot like when Caramel's puppies were born, except this was a person. Doctor MacKenzie had me wrap the afterbirth in a towel so he could take it along with him. He checked it over ever so carefully. He said he didn't want any of it missing 'cause that could make Mrs. Fenwick hemorrhage.

After it was all over he took us all home and told the Uncles the whole story. This was another one of those times when they opened the brandy bottle and had a glass. Mrs. Ruffles gave Judith and I lemonade in tall glasses to celebrate. The Uncles thought it was quite an experience, but Uncle Jimmy Burr once again expressed concern that I would be on a "high horse" over it all! I told him he didn't need to worry; it was just one of those kind of things that keep happening to me. Besides, delivering a baby wasn't really all that hard if everything was going right. And I told them I had already decided that I was going to go to college to become a doctor. So there was no reason at all to be surprised. Someday it would all be in a days work.

Uncle George Lee said, "Hear! Hear!" and raised a toast to the occasion.

Uncle Jimmy Lee said, "hurmph!" Doctor MacKenzie said I could be his partner any day.

The trip to Starved Rock is not so exciting by comparison, but it was a lot of fun. We climbed up and down rocks all day and read up on the history of the Illinois Indians. We learned how one tribe of Indians starved out another tribe at the top of this rock. That's how Starved Rock got it's name. It was real interesting. Judith said she had an absolutely marvelous time and that she has never enjoyed herself so much as she has in Talbotsville. I haven't heard one word about Bobby Vickers at all, but she still does carry on about Uncle Jimmy Burr. I told her I thought she had a crush on him, but she said, "Absolutely not! I just think he is a wonderful example of what a gentleman should be." I told her to be very careful, 'cause if Uncle Jimmy Burr hears her talking this way it will not be me who gets big headed about themselves. Of course, Judith got all upset about me saying this about Uncle Jimmy Burr.

The wedding plans are coming right along. The big day will be the second Sunday in September. Mrs. Ruffles is already putting up special goodies for the occasion. She is going to bake the wedding cake and decorate it with real flowers. I've never heard of doing that, but then lots of things are different here than they are in Evanston. Judith thinks it sounds "absolutely wonderful!"

Personally, I am getting tired of hearing Judith rave about how she feels so "absolutely" about everything. She got mad at me for saying that, so she is off with India Ingrid and has left me to pick beans, carrots, and beets by myself. I guess I will have to be more careful of what I say 'cause it does get boring to be in the garden all by myself. Mrs. Ruffles says I can't make Judith stay home and help 'cause she's a guest. I have learned my lesson and will be more polite in the future. Uncle Jimmy Burr says he certainly hopes so!

Judith came back early in the afternoon and said she had absolutely missed me a lot. Thank goodness I had the good sense not to make any remarks to her.

Caramel's puppies are just wonderful. For once I agree with Judith that they are *absolutely* the best looking dogs I have ever seen. I will always keep one puppy from every generation. Then it will be like having Caramel with me for always.

Love and kisses,
Amber Lee

P.S. I hope you let me keep Caramel and a pup when you come home. It would be cruel if you didn't!

2 August, 1959

Dear Mother,

It seems like so long since I wrote you the last time. We have all been very busy here. For one thing, there are a lot of showers for Aunt Griselda and Uncle George Lee. For another, there have been a bunch of quilting bees. You'll never guess what! Of course I will have to tell you 'cause I don't want to wait until you write me and ask, "What?" So, here it is. The quilting bees are to make a wedding quilt for Aunt Griselda, but the surprise is, you and Daddy are to get one, too.

Mrs. Weatherbee (her name reminds me of bees) says that because of grandfather disowning you for marrying Daddy, no one had the pleasure of giving you showers or a quilting bee. So now they are going to make up for it. I think that is a grand idea, so does Judith. We have both been going to them and taking part in the quilting. It is real interesting. Some of these ladies have been quilting for sixty-five years, ever since they were little girls. It is just absolutely amazing. (I think I'm getting a bad habit like Judith!) The ladies have told us that when we get married they will make a quilt for us, too. We were thrilled about it. Of course, I don't think that I will ever marry 'cause Uncle Jimmy Burr says, "Who would want to marry a bossy lady doctor like you?" Well, I can tell you I said a thing or two about that remark. Then he just threw back his head and laughed and laughed. He says he can get me every time. He tells me I am too serious and I bite on every joke. I tell him it is very hard to tell when he is serious or joking, so he needs to shape up. Judith is shocked when I talk with him this way, but I tell her he is my uncle and I can do as I please.

We have been so busy canning and preserving that I don't know what we are supposed to do next. Even the Uncles are busy with us every evening. The garden is two whole acres big, and there is so much stuff that I don't know anymore what is left to pick. We have even hired the Latimer twins to help out in the evenings. Mrs. Ruffles had a hired girl helping her in the inside kitchen and in the summer kitchen. I've never heard of a summer kitchen before, but the Uncles have one and it's where we are doing most of the canning now that it is hot outside. I suppose you know all about them, but I never heard of one in Evanston.

Judith and I are getting very good at making jam and jelly. India Ingrid says she has been making jelly since she was six years old. I don't know whether to believe that or not, but I know that we are learning how and have made about fifteen batches each. Mrs. Ruffles says it makes a wonderful Christmas present and has told Judith she can take lots of it home with her.

We went out and saw the new baby yesterday. Edith Amber is doing very well. She is a very pretty baby and her mother says she thinks Edith Amber looks a lot like me. I don't see how she can, being a baby and all, and not being related, but I suppose her mother sees something I don't. She is a happy little thing though, and she smiles a lot. I got to hold her and feed her a bottle when we went to visit. I told her that when she gets older I will take her for picnics at The Fairies' Parlor on her birthdays. I don't think I will ever go there again without thinking of her.

I was in the Uncles' store yesterday and everyone I met would stop and talk to me about Edith Amber. I think the whole county must know by now that I delivered a baby. I think this is another one of those occasions when I might have to write a story about it and sell it to the paper again. It's getting kind of hard trying to be nice when people say, "What will happen next?" I really don't want to be so famous that everyone points to me on the street. Judith thinks it's absolutely wonderful and she can't wait to get home to Evanston and tell everyone all about it. She even called her mother on the phone and told her.

We have a lot of things planned for the next two weeks 'cause after that Judith's mother and dad are going to drive down here and pick her up. They are going to go on a little vacation after that, and then it will be time for school to start again. I can hardly believe that summer is almost gone already. It seems like just yesterday that school let out, and now it is almost time to go back. I will be going to high school in Riverwood, the next town. It is a consolidated high school and I will have to take the school bus to get there. I've been feeling kind of nervous about it. But Uncle Jimmy Burr says there's nothing to it; you just wait for the bus, it comes, and you get on it and go to school. I told him that it's easy enough for him to say, but I'm the one meeting all the new people who start asking questions about delivering babies and sewing up dogs. He says, "Well then, you'll have to think of a new career!"

I just said, "Oh bother!" and walked away.

The new clothes arrived. They are very pretty. The dresses fit real nice, but they are a little short. Mrs. Ruffles has let down the hems, but she says, "You'll be out of these in no time; you're just like a weed!" I told her I hope I'm not the kind that makes her sneeze. She says, "You're starting to sound just like Jimmy Burr." I didn't say anything to her, but that remark sure made me stop and think.

Well, I am going to close now, but please be sure and write soon. I hope I will be a big sister by the time I hear from you again.

Love,
Amber Lee

20 August, 1959

Dear Mama,

I know the baby isn't supposed to be born until November. It's just that I get anxious about it. I will quit asking about it and just see how you are doing. Let me know so I can tell everyone. People are asking all the time. A person would think that no one ever has a baby in this town. Lots of folks talk about how nice you are, and that I look just like you.

Well, Judith has gone back home. She left a couple of days ago. Her parents came down and picked her up. They left for a few days of vacation in Wisconsin. Her mother said she could have one of the pups. Judith picked out the one that looks just like Caramel, so I will wait until the next litter is born to pick one to keep. Caramel is such a good mother. Aunt Griselda says she has never seen a dog so well behaved as Caramel. I am glad she is good 'cause she lives in my bedroom with me. It does get a little noisy at night, especially when the puppies get hungry. The Uncles tried to put Caramel in the back pantry with her puppies, but she cried so much they had to give in and let her come back to my room. Uncle Jimmy Burr says at this rate, no one will ever get a decent nights sleep again.

Mrs. Ruffles has been keeping me very busy since Judith went home. The garden has not slowed down one whit. (That's my new word for this week. Uncle George Lee says it comes from *whittle*.) I have been very busy with picking and washing vegetables. Canning has become a full time job for Mrs. Ruffles and Aunt Griselda. We have a hired girl to do the housework now. I asked the Uncles how we are saving anything if we have to hire all these people to help us do the work. All I get from them is that it is not a matter of saving money; it is a matter of "home canned tastes better!" They also pointed out that it is an expected source of income for some of the townspeople and they need it to make ends meet. It is not the same as Evanston at all.

I have had specific chores to do, and then Mrs. Ruffles lets me have some time for myself. Actually, I don't mind helping one bit. I've gotten used to it by now and since India Ingrid and Sarah Susan are doing the same thing at their houses, there is no time to go picnicking anyway. We have canned so many things that I have lost track. Mrs. Ruffles says they even put up some meat to have on hand for the unexpected.

I know it sounds like I am not doing anything but work. That is not true. In the evenings Sarah Susan and I go over to India Ingrid's house and sit on the porch. We usually play table games or just sit and talk. It is very interesting to talk about your dreams. India Ingrid wants to study in Europe. She is a very good artist and says that it is important to study the masters.

Sarah Susan is always very quiet when we get started on this subject, but she says her dream is to own a Paris fashion. Oh, Mama, I wish there was something to be done for her. She just gets more tired every day, and no one can do anything to stop it. Her daddy won't live a year; that's what Doctor MacKenzie says. I ask him why can't they go to a dry climate, but he just shakes his head and says not everyone has that luxury. Why should moving to a dry climate be a luxury?

I never knew anyone who was dying before. Sarah Susan never says anything about that, but I can tell she knows what is going to happen. She told me yesterday she wants to talk to me alone. I said I will come over and visit this weekend after church. India Ingrid is going to her grandmother's house for a birthday party, so she won't be home. If she didn't get invited she would feel left out, and we don't want to do that to her. I don't know what Sarah Susan wants to talk about, but I think it must be important.

Next week Aunt Griselda is going to take me shopping in Champaign-Urbana for a few more school items. She says that I have never been there, so she wants to take a day away and have some fun. I quite agree with her! She has been very busy too, getting ready for the wedding. I think there are a couple of things Aunt Griselda wants to buy for herself to wear on her honeymoon. They are going to go to New Orleans for a couple of weeks. You should hear Uncle Jimmy Burr on that subject. He says he surely doesn't know how in the world he will get by without Uncle George Lee for two whole weeks. Uncle George Lee gets red in the face and bites as hard on the teasing as I do. Uncle Jimmy Burr just sits and laughs when this happens. He says he can tell who I take after in this family. Well, I don't know for sure who I take after, but I think on the whole it's not Uncle George Lee.

Mrs. Ruffles just puts up with all of this as if nothing in the world is going on at all. She just sits and smiles and says it's purely wonderful to hear laughter in this house again.

You should see the cellar. It looks like a grocery store, plumb full of canning jars filled with different things. Of course, Mrs. Ruffles says a lot of it will go to a family in need and to several old people who are infirm. She says it is just as important to share the abundance from your garden as it is to share your purse. I never heard of that before, but it makes sense to me. There are bushels of all kinds of things: potatoes and squash, carrots and pumpkins, cucumbers and dried beans. Mrs. Ruffles says that after the beans are fully dry we will shell them and store them in jars. I guess the last thing that we put up is apples. It sounds like apple picking is a big event, too. People get together and make apple cider and there is a big apple festival and a dance. It is held when the September moon is full. I guess Uncle George Lee and Aunt Griselda will miss it this year 'cause they won't be here. Uncle Jimmy Burr says we will dance to fiddle music without them. And besides, they probably won't even notice they've missed it.

Well, I will say adios. (I have just met the new Mexican family in town and I am learning a few new words in Spanish.) Write to me soon.

Love and kisses,
Amber Lee

25 August, 1959

Dear Mother,

I just had to write to you and talk about Sarah Susan. I went over to visit her and I feel so bad I just don't know what to do. She isn't going to go to school with the rest of us this year. Doctor MacKenzie has prescribed rest for her, and lots of special foods and vitamins and minerals. He says it is just too much for her to go to another town, even if it is riding on a school bus. She doesn't have enough strength and he wants to conserve what she has left. I came home all scared about what is going to happen to her. Doctor MacKenzie never tells me outright, but I just know she is not going to live very much longer. I don't know if I can bear it 'cause I love her so much, and she is one of the very best friends I have ever had.

Oh, Mother, I wish you and Daddy were here. This is such a terrible time for me, but I know I have to have courage 'cause Sarah Susan said I was such an inspiration for her. I know that I can't let her down and act like a coward in front of her. I came home and cried. Even Caramel knew something terrible was wrong, but she wasn't able to help at all. Please write to me and tell me what to do.

Sarah Susan has asked me to bring all her school work home for her. She is going to have a special teacher that will come to her house once every week and then I am supposed to come over every day and pick up her homework. I will do everything that I can to help. I just wish that I could make her well. I think it is just terrible that she cannot go and live in a different climate 'cause that might save her life. I have read there is some medicine for TB. How come she can't get any of it? I think Uncle Jimmy Burr has an idea of what is wrong 'cause he just put his arm around me and gave me a big hug for no reason. Later he said something to me about how sometimes in life there are things we all have to accept, even though we don't understand them.

So, Mama, every night when I pray for you and Daddy and the Uncles, I pray for Sarah Susan, too. I am going to talk plainly to Doctor Mackenzie about this. In the meantime I will do my best and help Sarah Susan all I can.

I miss you and Daddy so much, please write soon.

Love,
Your daughter,
Amber Lee

10 September, 1959

Dear Mother,

School has started! Unfortunately, there is once again some good news and some bad news! The good news is wonderful. The wedding is next weekend and I am going to be the maid of honor for the bride. I am so thrilled I can hardly stand it. Aunt Griselda bought me an absolutely gorgeous taffeta. It is a lovely shade of peachy-pink and looks absolutely wonderful on me. We bought it the day we went shopping together in Champaign. That was one exciting day I can tell you, 'cause it's the first bigger city I've seen down here. It's only forty-five miles to go there, so Aunt Griselda says if I'd like to we can go more often when she comes home from her honeymoon. I said I thought that would be fun. We could even take India Ingrid along with us, and bring something special home for Sarah Susan.

She is doing better, Sarah Susan I mean. Rest is agreeing with her and I can see a big difference. Her color is not so pale as it was and she doesn't cough quite as much. Her school work is going well, too. I am very diligent in bringing her homework back to school with me.

I guess I'd better tell you about the bad news. One of the new boys that I met on the bus was teasing me a lot. Actually, I put up with a lot from him, but the second day after we got off of the bus in Riverwood, he pushed me down on the ground and threw my papers all over. Now some of them were Sarah Susan's and I know how hard it is for her to do her homework, so this made me very mad. The papers blew away because of the wind and I knew both of us would have to redo our homework. He kept laughing at me and pushing at me when I tried to get up. He said, "You think you're so smart 'cause you sewed up a dog." He said if it had been him, he would have killed it and put it out of its misery. Oh, Mama, I'm so ashamed of what happened next, but I know I have to tell you. The boy kept on laughing and when he turned around to walk away, I got up in a flash and ran at him with my head down. I butted him right in the stomach with my head. That's not all though—this is the bad part—when he doubled over from losing his breath, I let him have it with what James MacKenzie describes as a right cross to his jaw. Well, Mama, that boy went down like a load of bricks. And this is truly the very worst part; I broke his jaw.

The Uncles were very upset. Doctor MacKenzie was the most understanding. He just said that people with glass jaws shouldn't go around picking on people smaller than them. He says that occasionally the underdog rears up and fights back and sometimes even wins fights.

Well, the long and the short of it is, I was suspended from high school for a day. I had to go in and see the principal with the Uncles and explain myself. It was only after I told him how I wouldn't have done anything nearly so terrible if it had just been my homework, but when the boy had destroyed Sarah Susan's, well, I just couldn't let that go. I said that I hoped he understood; it was the principle of the thing and I didn't have any regrets; except I really hadn't wanted to hurt the boy. I said that usually I wasn't nearly so aggressive, and I would try not to let it happen again. Of course, I did tell him I expected that boy to let me alone in the future. He said he didn't think I had to worry about that; he had already talked to him. The boy, his name is Tom Deane, said he was truly sorry about the fight and it wouldn't happen again. He told the principal he wanted to see me and could I come visit him at the hospital? I told the principal I would think about it.

I can't imagine what in the world we would talk about, since everyone is saying I beat up a boy!

Well, that's all the news for now. I will write after the wedding and tell you how that goes.

Love you lots,
Amber Lee

25 September, 1959

Dear Mother,

The wedding was absolutely a dream. I've never been to anything so elegant. Aunt Griselda had two attendants, me as Maid of Honor, and her friend Marthe, from Riverwood. It went off without a hitch, even though Uncle Jimmy Burr said he expected someone to stand up and contest the groom's right to marry the bride. He even told me later, after a glass of brandy, that he thought of hiring someone to do it. The only reason he didn't was 'cause he said weddings are sacred trusts, and he didn't think he should interfere. I am certainly glad that he didn't do anything foolish. Uncle Jimmy Burr does have a rather strange sense of humor sometimes.

Everyone from Talbotsville was there. I don't think there was a face I did not see. Uncle George Lee had invited lots of his business associates from other places, too. Some of the salesmen from the big companies came, as well as a bunch more Talbot cousins that I never heard of before the wedding.

I met your auntie from Urbana. Actually, she says she is your great aunt, your grandfather's youngest sister. She has also got a big sense of humor, and I noticed she and Uncle Jimmy Burr had their heads together most of the morning. They made a lot of phone calls and then talked with a lot of the guests. I knew something was going on, but I didn't know what. We didn't find out until late that night. Auntie Lucy's husband was an engineer on the Panama Limited before he died. That's the night train that travels to New Orleans. She and Uncle Jimmy Burr had the Panama make a whistle stop in Talbotsville to pick up the bride and groom. It was the talk of the town for the whole week. I guess the last time the Illinois Central passenger train stopped here was when a passenger had a bad appendicitis attack and they had to let her off to have emergency surgery at Riverwood Hospital.

Anyway, it was a terribly exciting day. I wonder if my wedding day will even compare to this. I don't know how it could match this for excitement or fun! Of course, Uncle Jimmy Burr and Aunt Lucy assured me that in all probability I would never marry, as doctors should be dedicated to their patients. I told them, "Hooey!"

There are lots of presents to catalog, as Mrs. Ruffles puts it, so that we send the proper thank-yous to all the guests. I guess we will be busy with that for a while. Aunt Lucy will be here for the next several weeks to help. She says that at her age, traveling is a serious business, and when you arrive somewhere you plan on staying awhile and resting.

Well, I don't know about resting; I don't think Aunt Lucy has spent one entire day in this house with nothing to do. In her travels she has visited every mortal person in this town, as well as some of the immortal ones at the cemetery. As Uncle Jimmy Burr puts it, "There is no grass growing under her feet!"

She has invited me to come and visit her this winter at her house in Urbana. She says it is a big old Queen Anne house with lots of cubby holes and attics. It's a lot like this one, she says. Aunt Lucy says she has a real big yard, fenced in with a wrought iron rail and tall brick columns. It sounds real fancy. She said it was built for one of the railroad executives and his wife, but the wife died and so he sold it instead. Aunt Lucy says Uncle Raymond had "a bit put by," so he bought it as an investment. They lived there ever since, and never did sell it 'cause Uncle Raymond loved the wonderful view of the river from the house.

It sounds like an exciting and romantic place. I hope the Uncles will let me go. She says she thinks Thanksgiving would be a wonderful time for a visit. I guess I think so, too. What do you think?

Aunt Lucy says this house looks wonderful as well. She's certainly right about that, since the redecoration. Mother, it looks like a new place. Aunt Griselda even had some remodeling done in the summer house. It's just beautiful out there. There's even a guest bedroom, in case we have more visitors that we can put up in the house. It's absolutely neat! The view from my bedroom is perfect; I can see all the way to the woods, by Merton Crumbie's house. Oh, I remember what I was going to ask you; is Merton Crumbie my uncle now that his sister married Uncle George Lee? I need your answer as soon as possible. I would ask here, but I don't want anyone to think I am ignorant!

I hope everyone there is okay. Your visit to Paris sounds fabulous! Oh, how Sarah Susan would envy you. Can you send her a postcard from the Eiffel Tower? I would appreciate it very much.

Love and Kisses,
Amber Lee

10 October, 1959

Dear Mama,

The Fall Festival was a wonderful success! I never knew there were so many things you could do with apples. I even have a dried apple doll. Mrs. Ruffles made it for me as a keepsake. I think I shall treasure it always. Judith and her parents drove down here for the weekend to pick up the puppy and they stayed for the festival.

Judith's mother says it's the best time she has had in many years. She says it reminded her of growing up in rural Wisconsin, and now she wonders why they ever left there. It was very interesting to listen to Judith's mother and dad discuss this 'cause he had to keep reminding her how many things she likes about Chicago. I have started to think about what it will be like to go back home. You and Daddy will be home in January and then I will have to move back to Evanston. It seems strange to even think about it now. I miss my friends, like Judith, but really I don't know how I will be able to leave here and not see the Uncles and Aunt Griselda every day. Mrs. Ruffles assures me that I will adjust. She uses that word a lot. She says children are very adjustable. I told her that I did not necessarily agree with her, but she says that when I grow up and have reached her age, I will see just how much more adjustable children are than adults. She says, for example, look at Uncle Jimmy Burr and how set he is in his ways. Every day, rain or shine, he eats oatmeal for breakfast. She says that even if the sun rose in the west one morning he would look at it, not bat an eye, and just ask for his bowl of oatmeal, please.

I think she is right about him, but I still disagreed about my being so adjustable. I think the person who adjusts a lot is Aunt Lucy. She is remarkable. We sit and talk about all kinds of things in the evenings. It is very entertaining to have conversations with her 'cause she knows so much about so many different things. She has traveled a lot, too. She and Uncle Raymond traveled all over the United States after he retired from the railroad. She says it was *absolutely* (Aunt Lucy picked up a certain word from Judith, too.) the best year of her life, except for the one when she met Uncle Raymond!

In the evenings we sit around the porch and play some table games, like Monopoly or rummy. It is interesting that when India Ingrid and I talk with Mrs. Ruffles or Aunt Lucy, it is just like talking to our friends. They don't seem any older sometimes, especially when we are talking about serious things. One evening we started to talk about the fact that Sarah Susan is going to die. We forgot all about the Monopoly game and sat and talked instead.

I talked a lot about how I felt about death and that it scared me a lot. I was so surprised when Aunt Lucy and Mrs. Ruffles said they felt the same way. Aunt Lucy says what really helps her a lot when she gets afraid is she thinks about this being God's world. She says when she thinks about all the things God does for us, especially sending Jesus to us, she feels a whole lot better. She told me you can't be afraid and believe in God at the same time. I thought about that a lot and I think she's right.

I will have to talk with Pastor Buckley about it. I think it would help if I could understand why God doesn't want Sarah Susan to live anymore. I pray and pray about it, but Sarah Susan just gets sicker and sicker. I get so sad; I start to cry and think it just isn't fair.

Well, I will close now. Aunt Lucy is going home next week, so I don't want to spend all the last remaining days writing letters. I am glad that you are feeling so good. It doesn't seem possible that in a little more than a month I will have a new baby brother!

Write to me soon.

Love,
Amber Lee

25 October, 1959

Dear Mom and Dad,

Aunt Lucy is gone home and Uncle George Lee and Aunt Griselda are home. They said they had an absolutely wonderful time in New Orleans. The only thing is, on the way home the *City of New Orleans* did not make a whistle stop in Talbotsville. Instead they had to get off in Champaign-Urbana.

They did stop and see Aunt Lucy for an overnight. I guess it is all set to go there for the Thanksgiving weekend. I am really looking forward to it.

Tom Deane is back in school and he has been as good as his word. I think he could end up being a very good friend, especially if we lived closer. However, as Doctor MacKenzie pointed out, if I had too many good friends that lived in Talbotsville, I would never have time to work for him on Saturdays or do any of my school homework.

I am taking a lot of subjects in school: English 1, Spanish 1, Algebra, Civics, Art, and Phys. Ed. It's a lot of studying every day. I need to keep up my grades 'cause Doctor MacKenzie says I won't get into the university if my grades are low. He says you have to be "top drawer" to get into medical school at the University of Illinois. So I am working hard every day with my homework.

I am writing a paper for Civics on Abraham Lincoln and the aspects of his life that affected his presidency. I have been doing a lot of research. I never knew he had such a problem with *melancholia*; that's what his peers called his serious nature. Some of the historical writers say he was very depressed at times and dreamt about his own death. It sounds kind of spooky to me. I'm glad I don't have those kind of dreams. I'm having enough trouble with the dreams I've got, like being late to school and forgetting my homework.

64

I don't get a chance to go to the football games on Saturday 'cause I don't want to give up my job. Doctor MacKenzie takes me on rounds with him sometimes, and now I do some assisting with him in the office. Once in awhile he lets me open sterile packages of sutures for him, or I can scrub up a wound before he treats it. He says I have a very light touch and just maybe I could learn to be a doctor.

We finished picking all of the walnuts last week, so finally we are done with canning, preserving, and pickling. Now that it's all done and I go down to the root cellar and look at the rows and rows of jars, I feel real proud. It still doesn't seem to me as though it could really be finished; it got to be such a regular chore.

Aunt Griselda has hired an extra helper for Mrs. Ruffles. She says that it's about time that Mrs. Ruffles enjoys life more and works less. So she takes her out calling in the afternoons. Mrs. Ruffles grumbled to begin with, but now I think she is enjoying her freedom a whole lot. She says she is seeing people that she has not seen in a whole year.

I am glad that Mrs. Ruffles is having more fun. I guess when I came to live with the Uncles I just took her for granted. I never thought about how much work it must be for her to have me here. Yesterday I surprised her with a special gift that I made myself, just for her. It took me six months to do it, but I'm real proud of it. I embroidered a tea set for her and she and Aunt Griselda are going to have some ladies from church over for tea, to show it off to them. She was real tickled with it.

It sounds like you and Daddy are almost done with your project over there. Are you going to be able to come home earlier that you thought? Write to me and let me know. I will close for now.

Love and Kisses,
Amber Lee

Dear Mama,

It has been a terrible week! I have so much to tell you that I don't know where to start. First of all, I was called into the principal's office again. Uncle Jimmy Burr was aghast at the idea, but then when I told him the whole story he came to my aid! Mama, freedom of speech is not so alive and well in Talbotsville! This is what happened. Remember, I told you I was writing a paper on Abraham Lincoln and the effect his *melancholia* had on his presidency? Well, I wrote a first rate paper on this topic; it took me three weeks of work and research. I had all kinds of documentation from Lincoln biographers and everything, but it was still a disaster!

My teacher tore it up! I never even got a copy of it back from him. He stood up in front of the class and starting talking about a student who was not very patriotic. He said she had maligned the greatest president that ever was in Washington. He kept talking about the audacity of this young woman and how could she say such terrible things about Abraham Lincoln. It was terrible. Then he said he was giving this young woman a failing grade and that she had better be very careful in the future 'cause he did not like it one bit, that someone so young should be so opinionated. Then he tore up my paper and threw it away!

He passed all the other papers out to my classmates, so it was very obvious who the opinionated young woman was. That was when I had my tizzy-fit! I told that teacher a thing or two about how I had researched very carefully. And I also remarked that if he thought *I* was opinionated, how about all those biographers I was quoting!? When it was all over I had told him I thought *he* was the opinionated person, not me, and that I thought he had no right to tear up my paper and throw it away in the trash. When I tried to retrieve it from the waste paper basket, he pushed me away and sent me to the principal's office. He said I should be expelled for being a bad influence on the other kids! Oh, mama, it was a terrible, terrible time. I don't know how I would have survived this embarrassment if it hadn't been for Tom Deane. He got right up and went out of the class with me. Mr. Reilly was even screaming at him. He told Tom if he left, he could never come back either. We both went to talk to the principal, but he was gone for the afternoon. So the school secretary said she didn't have any choice but to send us home. She had to call the Uncles to come and get me.

Oh Boy, Mama. I never saw Uncle Jimmy Burr so mad at anybody as he was at me. But I kept telling him what the paper was about and how I had done all this research and all. All of a sudden he looked at me and said, "Do you mean to tell me that what he berated you about is recorded biographical fact? You got your information from the library resources? Is this the research paper you've been working on for three weeks? Is this the paper you've been dragging all those books home for? Is that the paper?"

Well, all of a sudden he wasn't mad at me anymore. He was furious at my teacher and kept carrying on about my rights to say what I thought. Actually, Mama, it was quite a history lesson 'cause Uncle Jimmy Burr kept talking about the right to "Freedom of Speech." When we got home he called Uncle George Lee and told him he thought he had better come home 'cause their niece had been expelled from school for exercising her rights as an American citizen. Oh, Mama, it was something, the way he carried on about it.

Uncle Jimmy Burr was just like the white knight rescuing the damsel in distress. Of course, Aunt Griselda and Mrs. Ruffles got involved too, and before I knew it, half the neighbors knew what had happened.

When Uncle George Lee got home he said, "Of course, Lincoln had a problem with depression. Who wouldn't if they were dealing with a civil war and a sickly wife?" It was at that point that Aunt Griselda started to giggle, and then it moved on to outright laughing. She laughed so hard that she had to sit down and hold her sides. She said it was one of the funniest sights she ever saw, when Uncle George Lee started talking so rationally about Lincoln's "problem with melancholia." She said here we were talking about the whole thing as if Lincoln was a neighbor who was having a problem with his family life, and then started having problems on the job.

Mrs. Ruffles kept on defending me and saying, "No teacher has the right to tear up my girl's papers. I don't care what he thinks. I'm going to give him a piece of my mind." It was at this point that Uncle Jimmy Burr got the giggles. He said later it was because he really began to picture *pieces* of Mrs. Ruffles mind scolding the teacher.

Anyway, Mama, the next day we all went to the principal's office and talked it over. The Uncles, Aunt Griselda, Mrs. Ruffles (who insisted she wasn't going to be left out, as she was practically a member of the family), and me.

We were there for two hours. The teacher was called in to meet with us and to talk over the problem. He absolutely insisted that he would do the same thing in the future. He said he felt that children should not be writing such despicable things about such a famous man. After all, Lincoln was the most famous citizen of Illinois, and this was the "Land of Lincoln." Uncle Jimmy Burr said "That's true. However, what really makes Lincoln such an exceptional person was the very fact that he was called upon to act on the most pressing national issues, like the Civil War and slavery, while at the same time he was dealing with his own very difficult personal problems."

Uncle Jimmy Burr insisted that Mr. Reilly apologize to me for tearing up my paper and embarrassing me in front of my class. He said that Mr. Reilly had violated my rights to freedom of speech and that what I had written was factual. He also said that Mr. Reilly should give me a decent grade for the paper, as it was "quite a good piece of work."

Mr. Reilly said he wouldn't do it. It was a real stalemate. The principal said this was a good time to take a little break, so he sent us out of his office for a few minutes. When we came back it was decided that I was going to be placed in another Civics class with a different teacher. I asked if Tom Deane would be, too. After all, he had gotten into trouble on my account. And Mr. Reilly was going to give him a failing grade as well because he stuck up for me. The principal said he'd think about it.

I was sure glad when all that was over! It makes Halloween pale by comparison. We had a real good time on Halloween. Aunt Griselda organized a party for all of us. We went out "trick and treating" early in the evening and then we came home for the party. Sarah Susan came as an Indian princess and India Ingrid was a clown. I dressed up as a doctor. Doctor MacKenzie got me some white surgical gowns and a mask, so I wore this out for "tricks or treats." We got a lot of candy, but Mrs. Ruffles locked it up in the pantry. She says it has to be doled out to me, or my teeth will rot.

There were some tricks that night, too. Deuteronomy Fenwick's outhouse was tipped over. (They thought it was the Latimer twins, but they worked late and then came over here.) Also Merton Crumbie's old wagon was put up on top of his machine shed. I can't figure out how that was done, but Uncle George Lee just smiles knowingly and doesn't answer me. (What did you and the Uncles do as kids on Halloween?) All in all, it was a wonderful time. We bobbed for apples and Aunt Griselda and Uncle George Lee set up a haunted house in the barn. It was really quite spooky. We all had a great time.

Mrs. Ruffles and everyone else asks if the baby is born yet. I keep telling them that you will let us know as soon as it happens!

Keep writing; I really like getting your letters. Pretty soon we will all be together again.

Love,
your daughter,
Amber Lee

30 November, 1959

Oh Mama, I'm so excited I can't stand it! Twins! That is the most wonderful news I ever heard. Two sisters! Wow! I thought it was for sure going to be a baby brother, but this is even better! The whole town of Talbotsville is talking about it. What a surprise!

I like their names, Heptzibah and Rachel. Thank you for the telegram. That's the talk of the town, too. Hardly anyone ever gets a telegram here, so it was really something to get it. I wish I was there with you. It's really hard to imagine what it's like to be a big sister when the babies aren't here to hold. When are you coming home? It was really exciting to hear that you had the babies out on the dig site. It's a good thing that your host family knows about having babies. It sounds like Mrs. Gottlieb is a lot like Mrs. Ruffles. She certainly sounds wonderful and knows what to do in a crisis.

Which baby is older? Everyone is asking the same things I am asking you, so you need to send an answer. Mrs. Ruffles wants to send baby gifts, but I told her by the time the packages got there you would probably be gone. I said that you and Daddy would come down to Talbotsville to show off the babies, and take me home to Evanston. She has this funny look on her face when I say this. I think that she is starting to miss me already.

I try not to think about not living in Talbotsville. I remember when I first came and thought it was such a hicktown and everyone was socially backward. I can remember the first time I saw the Latimer twins coming to school with no socks. I thought they were just being piggy and jerks. It never occurred to me they were poor and couldn't afford socks. When it really got cold, I guess their father would buy two sets at a time and go without something else.

Uncle Jimmy Burr was mad at me all the time back then; now I understand a lot of things about being poor. Last week we took the canned goods to the family the Uncles help out. They're wonderful people that live way out, almost fifteen miles from here. I guess they had a son the Uncles grew up with and he was killed in Korea. They are real poor, but they have a small piece of property attached to their old farm. They live in the old farmstead, but they are too infirm to do any gardening. The Uncles always make sure they have what they need to get along. Actually, I think the Uncles pay all their bills too.

Mrs. Miller—that's the lady of the house—makes quilts. Hers are a lot different than the quilting bee ones though. She makes hers out of tiny scraps of material, and when she is done they are absolutely fabulous. She doesn't make a pattern or anything, but they still end up symmetrical, and the colors balance beautifully. She says she has been making quilts since she was old enough to hold a needle. Uncle George Lee and Aunt Griselda were given one for a wedding present and they say they are afraid to use it. Uncle George Lee says making these quilts is a dying art form. I never thought of quilts being works of art, but I am beginning to understand what he is talking about.

The house is real different, too. The center of it is an old log cabin. It's the oldest part of the house. Now it holds the kitchen and a parlor and one upstairs bedroom. Two other parts of the house came later, so the rest of the upstairs is reached by a second stairway. It's real neat! The place looks like it could be a picture in a history book. Mr. Miller is still able to feed a few chickens and geese, and they have a dog and three cats. The cats are all old ones 'cause the Uncles had them fixed so they couldn't have babies. Anyway, this place is really something.

When I asked Mrs. Miller how she found so many antiques, she laughed and asked which ones I was talking about. She says they aren't antiques; they are her pieces of furniture from when she was first married. Her dining room furniture is mahogany. She has a big round table with claw feet. I never saw one that wasn't oak, so this is a first. She says you see more mahogany the farther south you go. She has some Hepple-white pieces, too. They are so beautiful. She says she inherited a lot of her furniture when her grandmother died. Wow, Mama, it must be very old!

She has pictures of relatives from the Civil War period. She says one of the men is her grandfather. He was an officer in the Union Army. She said that was very hard for him though 'cause he had a brother who was in the Confederate Army. She said after the war was over it was many years before they spoke to each other. That sounds so sad. Anyway, it was like getting a very interesting history lesson from someone who was almost there.

She says I should come back with the Uncles and visit at Christmas time 'cause I would probably like all the funny old ornaments that she uses on the tree. I said I would like to do that, so we set a date to visit and she will have us all come to dinner and celebrate. I think that would be so exciting. Mrs. Miller said if I wanted to, I could bring a couple of friends. She said a girl my age might get bored with just old folks, so I should bring along some company. I almost jumped for joy 'cause I was thinking how much Sarah Susan would like it here. She likes old things and antiques. Her strength is not good, but she can still go places if you take her in a car. So I guess we will be able to bring her along.

Keep writing and let me know all the news about the babies. I hope you have someone helping you take care of them 'cause from what Mr. Latimer says, twins can be an awful chore!

Love,
Amber Lee

15 December, 1959

Dear Mama,

I would have written last week, but everything got so busy that I just didn't have time. This will be the last letter I send to you in Jerusalem. From now on I will send them to the New York address you sent me. It is so exciting that soon you will be on your way home. I just can't tell you how wonderful it will be to see you and Daddy again. At the beginning of the year I thought that this time would never arrive, but it seems like just last week that I came to Talbotsville for the first time. Isn't it funny how it seems like that?

I don't know what to tell you first. I guess I'd better begin with the dress from Paris. It was absolutely the most beautiful dress I have ever seen. The color is perfect; I have never seen a dusky rose so vibrant. The shoes were almost a perfect fit and they match exactly. I don't understand how they can do that so well. This is the part I don't know if you will understand, so here goes. I gave the dress to Sarah Susan. It's not that I didn't love the dress the minute I laid eyes on it; I did. It's just that . . . well, remember when I told you that her greatest wish was to own a dress from Paris? Well, now she does.

I took it over to her house to show it to her and somehow she misunderstood and thought it was for her, from you and Daddy. She knew that I had told you how much she dreamed about owning a fashion from Paris. So she thought it was for her. The funny part is, the minute she got so excited about this gift from you, I knew that it really should belong to her. So, in that split second I told the biggest lie I have ever told. I said you and Daddy sent it special for her for Christmas. I hope you won't be mad at me, but I just had to do it. It fits her perfectly and if I didn't know better, I'd think it really *was* made for her. The shoes fit her, too. I have to admit the shoes did pinch me a little, but I could have stretched them out enough to wear. Anyway, that is what happened and I think Sarah Susan has her greatest wish. She says she will wear it for all the Christmas celebrations, and she even wore it to the Millers' house for dinner.

The dinner was wonderful. We had roast turkey with every kind of trimming you can imagine. Mrs. Miller is a fabulous cook. She is even better that Deuteronomy Fenwick's wife, and I thought she was the best cook I ever met. Mrs. Ruffles is really good at it too, but there are some things that she does not like to make, so they never taste right to me. The turkey dressing had oysters in it. Uncle Jimmy Burr says it is his favorite kind in all the world. I tried it, but I think those oysters are something I will have to acquire a taste for over time. We also had corn meal dressing. I never dreamt corn meal could taste so good.

When we went to Aunt Lucy's for Thanksgiving, she had all kinds of new things that I tried, too. I'll tell you about that dinner when you get home. I will just say this, I think Aunt Lucy is going to try to give you her house. She kept talking about how nice it would be if you came to Champaign-Urbana to live. She says Daddy could teach at the University of Illinois, instead of at Northwestern. Don't be surprised if she brings up the subject to you.

Anyway, the dinner at the Miller's house was wonderful. India Ingrid and I went for a long walk in the fields. I brought along stout shoes to do that, and so did she. I have decided that you have to take long walks after some of these country meals or you would gain a lot of weight from all the goodies. Sarah Susan stayed in the parlor and listened to old Caruso records on this incredibly ancient phonograph. I never saw one like it, but she said that it is very valuable and she wanted to listen to it. She wore the new dress and she looked so pretty that I thought I was going to start crying out loud. India Ingrid and I talked about it on our walk. I don't know how we will be able to stand it, if she dies.

India Ingrid and I talked for a long time with Pastor Buckley about Sarah Susan. He said he had talked with her too. He says she knows she is going to die, and that she has accepted it. He said it is much harder on her family and her friends at this point. He also told us her father will not live much longer either, so her mother and brothers and sisters will need a lot of help in the coming months. I told him I would do everything I could to help. Oh, Mama, it is so hard to understand this. I know I have told you that before, but it is still true. I don't know what I will do when the time comes.

Pastor Buckley and I talked a lot about our beliefs about life. He says that I seem to have a very clear philosophy of life for my age. I'm not sure what he means by that, but it sounded very serious and complimentary. I do know that I have some opinions on what life is all about. Do you think that's what he is talking about? I guess I should ask him.

I am helping with the Christmas program at church. The sunday school kids always have a service on Christmas Eve. It is exciting to be part of planning it. The readings will be from the King James Bible, the Chapter of Luke. I think those readings are so beautiful. Someday I will read these same things to my children on Christmas Eve. Do you think when I am older I will remember what it feels like now, on Christmas? I hope so.

Well, I am going to close now. Pretty soon we will all be together again. I want to see my new sisters so bad that I can hardly stand it. Give them lots of kisses from me.

Love you very much and miss you,

Amber Lee

26 December, 1959

Dearest Mother,

I don't know why it is, the saddest things and the happiest things seem to come together. Christmas Eve was so beautiful and the program turned out perfect. We had a live manger scene (this was my idea), and the Sunday School children had so much fun planning it. India Ingrid and Sarah Susan and I spent the four days before Christmas rehearsing all the kids so they would be letter perfect. They were, too! Sarah Susan said it was the most perfect Christmas she ever had in her life.

She wore the dress for Christmas Eve and she looked like a princess in it. Pastor Buckley took flash pictures of the three of us by the Christmas tree in church. I'm so glad he did because Sarah

Susan died late in the afternoon on Christmas Day. I'm still crying so much I can hardly write about it, but I felt that I needed to let you and Daddy know. You'll never know how much I will miss her or how glad I am that I gave her the dress.

She was so happy on Christmas and she said she had never felt so good before, not ever in her whole life. Her mother said she laid down for a nap in the afternoon and sometime during the nap God came and got her. Oh, Mama, I can hardly tell you in words how I feel, but I believe Pastor Buckley when he tells me this will pass. He says we can never be given something more painful than we can bear. I told him that I did not agree with him about that, but somehow I would come through it.

I can't tell you how much I will miss Sarah Susan. She really was so special, even more than Judith and India Ingrid. I think that must be because she saw things they didn't. Things like how beautiful the autumn trees are and how some special places in the forest have enchanted fairies in them. I could always share those kinds of thoughts with her, and she never laughed at me like some people would.

Sarah Susan's mother asked if I would mind if she was buried in the Paris frock. She says that Sarah Susan had never in her whole life looked as beautiful as she did in that dress. I told her I thought Sarah Susan would like it. The funeral will be tomorrow and I hope I can get through it okay. I'm afraid I will cry and cry and not be able to stop.

I'm going to say goodbye for now because I just can't write about it anymore, and I just haven't got the heart to tell you all about Christmas. It all seems to be so mixed up in my mind.

I will write you again in a few days. I hope that this is the right address in New York. It is the one you gave me in one of your earlier letters.

Please call me when you get back in the United States. I want to know you are home safe and sound with Daddy and the babies.

Love,
your daughter,
Amber Lee

1 January, 1960

Dear Mother,

It seems like the last week went by like a dream. Doctor MacKenzie and I had a long talk last evening on New Years Eve. We talked a lot about how people respond to tragedy. He says that even the worst sadness passes after a time, and that sometimes people feel guilty because they start to feel good again after someone dies. I asked him if he was talking about me because I had noticed I was feeling a whole lot better, and I told him how earlier that afternoon India Ingrid and I had started laughing about Caramel's antics.

In the middle of laughing I had started to feel real funny about it, and so I asked Aunt Griselda if it meant I didn't really love Sarah Susan. She said, "No. Life keeps on moving, even after people we love die. That's the way it's supposed to be." She had a funny look on her face when she said this, and then she told me, she had lost the man she was going to marry. She said he was killed in Korea. All of a sudden I knew she had been engaged to marry the Millers' son. For once I had sense enough not to ask a bunch of questions. Someday I know she will tell me all about it.

I didn't tell you much about Christmas around here in my last letter because I was feeling so bad about Sarah Susan, so I will tell you now.

Aunt Lucy came for Christmas and she is still here visiting. I think she is very lonely in Urbana and that's why she is going to stay until the middle of January. I think she wants to see you and Daddy, too. She keeps asking when you will arrive here in Talbotsville and I keep saying I don't know exactly when.

I wish you would write her a long letter and tell her when you will be here; then I can stop being the middle-man in my letters.

We had a lot of fun on New Years Eve. I wore my Christmas dress from Mrs. Ruffles. She made me the most elegant dress I have ever seen, except the one Sarah Susan wore. She is a wonderful seamstress and she spent the last week before Christmas making it as a surprise, since I gave Sarah Susan the one from you. It was a beautiful plaid—red, green, black, and white, very scottish looking. Mrs. Ruffles said the material came from Britain. The skirt was made from the plaid, but the top was made from the softest forest green velvet that I ever felt. It matched the green in the plaid. It was so soft it almost felt like fairies wings. The trim was velvet ribbons and hand made queen's lace.

Remember when I told you about Mrs. Ruffles making handmade lace, and how she was taught the pattern by the Queen of the Fairies? Well, that's the very lace pattern she used for my Christmas dress. She says that she wanted to create the most beautiful lace in the whole world. Well, I think she has succeeded in doing just that.

Well, Mother, I will close for now. This is the last letter I will be writing to you. Next week you will be home and we will finally see each other again. I hope that we never have to be apart again, ever.

I have so many things that I want to show you here in Talbotsville. I can hardly wait until you get here. If Daddy ever has to go on a sabbatical leave again, the next time I will be old enough to go with you. But I suppose by then I'll be too old to want to go along.

Here's all my love and kisses until I see you next week.

Love,
Amber Lee Johnston

P.S. I love you all.

I finished reading the last letter. Tears were coursing down my cheeks as I retied the ribbon around the letters. The year I lived in Talbotsville with the Uncles came back to me in a flood of memory. Sarah Susan's image in the Paris frock was so real I could almost touch it. As if to reinforce the memory a picture was the very next thing I found in the box. It was taken by Pastor Buckley on Christmas Eve, 1959. Our names were on the back in his handwriting: Amber Lee Johnston, Sarah Susan Adams, India Ingrid Harris. The Three Musketeers.

The years which have passed since that Christmas seemed like a week. All the events of my life stood out like special stations on the Illinois Central Railroad: moving into Aunt Lucy's house; watching the twins grow up; going to medical school and practicing with my father-in-law, Dr. Douglas MacKenzie; raising my family with my husband James; helping my father grieve my mother's death five years ago. All of it seemed like a series of sacred events.

Maybe that's what life is to me, a beautiful opportunity to experience the joy of loving others. Perhaps everything that happens to us is just the means to that end.

Pastor Buckley's comments on my philosophy of life were probably accurate, even that long ago. That year in Talbotsville which had started so painfully had become one of the biggest milestones in my life. I guess it taught me that the very thing you dread may be the best thing for you.

I stooped and picked up the next item in the box. It was the yellowed box of stationery which contained the last few sheets of puppy-decorated paper, and an old pencil that was still sharp. I picked them up and before I even stopped to think about what I was doing, I started to write.

15 October, 1989

Dear Mother,

So much has happened since I saw you last. The children are starting college now, James was just elected as the new judge at the county seat, my father-in-law has just retired and moved with his wife to the old Miller farmstead. Caramel's great-grand-daughter, that looked so much like her, just had pups . . .